. . . Handing Carol a towel, she said, "Would you do something for me tonight?"

"Sure. What is it?"

"I mean in bed." At Carol's anticipatory smile, Sybil added, "You may not like it."

"Leather? Whips? Bondage?" said Carol, highly amused. "Or do you want me to dress as a schoolgirl?"

"I want you to do absolutely nothing. I want you to leave it all to me."

Carol knew her expression had changed. Sybil said, "I said you mightn't like it."

Carol felt oddly defensive. "It's just that I . . ." She shrugged to complete the sentence.

"Humor me?"

This is ridiculous, thought Carol, realizing that she was apprehensive. She was used to dominance, to being in control. Even when Sybil was the initiator, Carol could command her own response, direct their love-making, maintain authority.

"Carol?"

After all, this is the woman I love, thought Carol. Aloud she said firmly, "You've got a deal."

THE DETECTIVE INSPECTOR CAROL ASHTON MYSTERY SERIES

COP OUT

THE 4th DETECTIVE INSPECTOR CAROL ASHTON MYSTERY

BY
CLAIRE McNAB

Bella
BOOKS

2003

Bella Books, Inc.
P.O. Box 10543
Tallahassee, FL 32302

First published 1991 by Naiad Press
Printed in the United States of America on acid-free paper

Editor: Katherine V. Forrest
Cover Design: Bonnie Liss (Phoenix Graphics)

ISBN 1-931513-29-5

For Jo

ACKNOWLEDGMENTS

I appreciate Katherine V. Forrest's contribution as editor more than my thesaurus can say!

Special thanks to Liz, and to Liz, for technical advice.

About the Author

Claire McNab is the author of eight Detective Inspector Carol Ashton mysteries: *Lessons in Murder, Fatal Reunion, Death Down Under, Cop Out, Dead Certain, Body Guard, Double Bluff,* and *Inner Circle.* She has also written two romances, *Under the Southern Cross* and *Silent Heart.* While a high school English teacher in Sydney she began her writing career with comedy plays and textbooks. In her native Australia she is known for her self-help and children's books.

For reasons of the heart, Claire is now a permanent resident of the United States, although she tries to visit Australia at least once a year and warmly recommends her country as a breathtaking vacation destination.

CHAPTER ONE

The hammer was an elegant black and silver. Its chrome shaft flashed with the first quick blow. A pause, filled with the sound of hard breathing, and then, bending, one final assault.

Urgent fingers felt for a pulse that flickered, then failed.

The refrigerator in the corner of the studio cut in, its motor humming loudly. Someone was outside, voice raised in querulous questions.

The hammer lay discarded, its bloody head bright against the cork tiled floor.

* * * * *

Detective Inspector Carol Ashton closed the folder
and leaned back in her chair to survey the
uninspiring beige walls of her office. But the stark
images of the children's bodies stayed clearly in her
mind. In this case, as in many others like it, the
murder-suicide followed a chilling pattern. A battle
for custody in the Family Court; the mother
"winning"; the father, apparently rational, taking his
children for his usual weekend visitation rights; the
discovery of the small pathetic bodies and their dead
father. And usually a note, intended to ensure the
surviving parent would suffer maximum guilt and
distress.

Carol tried, but failed, to imagine what it would
be like to identify her own son's body. And of course,
since her ex-husband had custody of David, if the
usual pattern were to be followed, *she* would have to
be the one to murder him and then commit suicide.
The enormity of such an act defeated her: to kill
one's own child.

A crime against nature — yet there was a
familiarity about this extreme domestic violence that
had blunted even the media's enthusiasm, so that it
took a case with a twist to make the front pages or
a quiet day on the television newsfront to have the
murder-suicide as a lead story. This small family
tragedy, reduced to photographs, reports and
statements in a folder on Carol's desk, had had no
special angle to make it particularly newsworthy, so,
apart from a blustering attack on the Family Court
by a television commentator who used identical
hyperbole whether discussing the court system,

2

political corruption or faulty labeling in supermarkets, this particular case had faded rapidly from public view.

Carol stared at the television set squatting blankly in the corner of her office, seeing her reflection distorted by the curvature of the screen. A woman in control, seated with authority behind a desk, blonde hair falling in disciplined lines, dark suit severe and businesslike, dealing with each case of violent death with calm efficiency. That was certainly the impression she had given earlier that morning on the seven o'clock news show.

Ongoing allegations of police inefficiency and the familiar calls from the State Opposition for a royal commission into possible corruption had forced the Commissioner into a public relations exercise. Carol usually found herself included in these efforts to create a positive public image because she had a high media profile and was skilled in handling the wiliest interviewer. Her appearance on the early morning television news program was ostensibly to discuss the use of new scientific techniques in crime detection, but was actually part of a well-organized effort to present the Force as efficient, reliable, and cleansed of all corrupt officers.

Although conscious of the importance of good public relations, Carol was impatient with the whole exercise. She felt stale, unmotivated. Even so, she had dealt efficiently with ill-informed questions from the smirking interviewer, who obviously saw himself as the match for any Detective Inspector, however media-wise she may be. They discussed the use of DNA profiling in a whole range of applications, from paternity suits to semen testing in sexual assault cases. As she knew he would, he then brought up the latest sensational crime, a gang-rape murder trial in which she had given evidence.

After delving into the brutal details, with a pause to emphasize some of the worst aspects of what had been a particularly hideous crime, he said challengingly, "So, Inspector, surely, as a woman, you must feel a need for revenge, a special reason to nail these men who savagely rape and murder?"

During the trial, when she had been giving evidence, her voice calm, dispassionate, she had looked over at the accused in the dock. There they sat, spruce in new suits, each with a studied look of clean innocence. Yet she knew what they had done and how they had done it. She remembered the rage that had put a momentary tremor into her voice. If it had been possible, at that moment she would have rid the world of their existence, exterminated them all.

To the interviewer she said, "As a police officer it's my job to gather evidence. The judge and jury decide each case. I make professional decisions on the likelihood of guilt, but I make no judgments. That's not my role, nor that of any police officer."

He had then veered off onto an unrelated issue about the small number of women in the upper echelons of the police hierarchy. Carol knew all the right things to say about equal opportunity and affirmative action and she heard her clear, confident voice repeating them with sincerity.

Afterwards the middle-aged woman removing Carol's television make-up had asked her about openings for young women in the Force. "My Debbie's that keen," she had said, her hands deftly applying face cream, "but her Dad and I told her it's still a man's world, specially in the police." She had looked thoughtfully over Carol's shoulder into the mirror where they both were reflected in the harsh light of the make-up room. "Debbie's seen you a lot on the telly," she said as Carol's green eyes met hers, "and she says *you've* done it, so why shouldn't she — but I said you were very good looking, beautiful, even, and that must have been a help. Was it, then?"

Carol had laughed off the question with a self-deprecating remark. Now she frowned. She had worked hard to get to be a Detective Inspector, but could she deny that her good looks at times had smoothed the way? And would she have had the media attention if she had been unremarkable, or even ugly?

And what was the point of considering how and why she had attained the rank of Detective Inspector? Or why the pleasure she took in her work had evaporated? She had seen colleagues experience burnout, the pressures of the job destroying peace of mind and health. She thought, I'd leave before I'd let that happen to me.

"Carol? See you a minute?"

She looked up to Mark Bourke's pleasantly homely face. He hadn't needed outstandingly handsome features to help his career — his success had been due to hard work and a low-key interviewing technique that could lull even the most suspicious into a dangerous complacency.

"The Darcy case," said Bourke as he handed her one of his carefully lettered folders. "And you don't need to get involved."

"No?" Unwillingly, she felt a glimmer of interest.

"As far as I can see it's open and shut. A nice neat case of fratricide."

He sat, self-consciously running his hand over his hair, which he had recently had cut so short it resembled a brown stubble.

Carol said, "How neat?"

Bourke's tone was appreciative. "Neatly executed and, I hope, about to be neatly solved. One or two nicely judged hammer blows to the head in order to dispatch her brother, then Charlotte Darcy waits in her studio, rolling her eyes and frothing at the mouth, to be found with body."

"I suppose you don't mean that literally. It's your usual colorful approach?"

Grinning, Bourke nodded. "So no froth." His tone became matter-of-fact as he continued, "The officers who answered the call from her husband yesterday afternoon said she was confused and incoherent. She was sitting on a tall work stool near the body with blood on her clothes and the hammer that is almost certainly the murder weapon on the bench beside her. One of the patrol officers asked her, 'Did you do this?' and he says she replied, 'I must have . . . I don't remember.'"

Carol played with her gold pen, pensively turning its smooth yellow cap with her fingertips. "Is she in custody?"

"Not yet. Her parents arrived with a tame psychiatrist — Dr. Naomi Reed, no less — shortly after I arrived."

"It's Nora and Keith Darcy, isn't it?"

Bourke looked surprised. "You know them?"

"They're friends of my Aunt Sarah, so I've met

them a few times. Keith Darcy's very influential in the Blue Mountains area, especially since Darcy Designs provides employment there and he's been the mayor of the local council for a couple of terms."

Bourke grunted. "He's a hard man — looks the type who usually gets what he wants. Charlotte Darcy's husband — Eric Higgins — faded into the background when his father-in-law arrived. Darcy tried leaning on me at first, insisting on seeing his son's body. That took the wind out of his sails and we had to help him out of the studio and into the house. Thought he'd collapse, but his wife sat him down and got him a brandy, all in the calmest way possible. It was funny, Carol, she didn't say a word the whole time and even when she looked at her dead son it seemed almost without interest."

"Shock takes different people different ways."

"How true," said Bourke flippantly. "It apparently drove Charlotte right around the bend. Dr. Reed, who had been examining her while I was dealing with her parents, stalked in to announce Charlotte was too ill to be interviewed and was being immediately admitted to her private clinic."

Carol leaned back to consider the situation. "So her parents brought a doctor, but no lawyer."

Bourke grinned. "The way their daughter was behaving, that seemed a wise choice."

Carol was used to Mark Bourke's irreverent attitude, but even so she felt nettled by his light-hearted comments about a mentally ill woman who apparently had murdered her brother. She said curtly, "How did Charlotte Darcy seem to you?"

Bourke considered. "When I first saw her she seemed detached, not with it, as though she wasn't

7

sure what had happened. Had a good look at her eyes and the pupils were dilated, but that, of course, could be aforementioned shock . . . or drugs. I had trouble getting her attention when I tried to get her to repeat her confession."

His cheerful tone provoked Carol. "You hadn't cautioned her."

Looking surprised at Carol's vehemence, Bourke said, "This was just the preliminaries, Carol. I'd just walked in the door. Anyway, she ignored me. I finally got some sort of response when I asked her how long she had been with her brother's body before her husband came in. Said she didn't know. Fingerprinted her and the husband and she watched the whole procedure with a sort of distant interest. Frankly, the woman was so far off the planet I don't think she really understood what she'd done."

Carol couldn't prevent a sharp note in her voice as she said, "So you've quite made up your mind Charlotte Darcy killed her brother?"

"I told you, it's open and shut. She's been going off the rails for the past few months, I gather, and she had a series of arguments, some very heated, with her brother Bryce over the last couple of weeks. As I see it, yesterday she snaps completely and beats his head in with the nearest adequate weapon. Look how it adds up, Carol." Enthusiastically, he counted off the points on his fingers. "First, I'll bet it's her fingerprints on the hammer. Second, it's almost certainly her brother's blood on her clothes. Third, they've been in violent conflict over the business. Fourth, Charlotte Darcy's acting like she's several sandwiches short of a picnic."

Leaning forward, he said persuasively, "And when

you put it all together you've got a murder at best, manslaughter at the least. And wheeling in a high society psychiatrist like Naomi Reed probably means the family will go for everything-went-to-black as a defense, and they'll probably get away with it too."

He frowned at her doubting expression. "Carol, you're trying to make this more complicated than it is. Maybe she's on drugs, maybe she's just crazy — either way, it's pretty clear what happened. I'm going to the Reed Clinic tomorrow to ask a few pointed questions. With a bit of luck I'll wrap it up in the next few days."

Carol felt a flicker of irritation at Bourke's cheerful appropriation of the case, a feeling that flared when he said, "I've brought Anne Newsome in on this one."

"Isn't she working with Ferguson on the Veringsky killing?"

Although her tone was neutral, Bourke looked at her closely. He said mildly, "That's pretty well completed, and Anne needs more experience in the field."

Carol wondered if his interest in the young Constable was more personal than professional. She was surprised at the jolt of resentment the idea gave her.

Leaning back, deliberately casual, she said, "Have you any time free this afternoon? I'd like to see the studio where Darcy was killed."

Bourke's face immediately became blank. But his voice was light as he shook his head. "Sorry, Carol, I'm tied up. Constable Newsome was with me yesterday, so she might be of help."

Carol noticed the transition from the informal use

of Anne to Constable Newsome. "Would you check with her, Mark, and also see if Charlotte Darcy's husband is available?"

After he had gone, Carol put the file to one side and dialed her home number, frowning as the answering machine clinked on, her own voice exhorting the caller to leave a message after the tone. She had expected Sybil to answer as she had Tuesdays off now that she was working as a part-time teacher.

Carol smiled at her own chagrin. Why should she expect everything and everybody to accommodate her wishes? She returned to the neatly labeled DARCY folder, skimming the contents. The victim, Bryce Darcy, had been married with two young sons. His wife had been eighty kilometers away in Katoomba at the time of the murder. She had been too distraught to be interviewed immediately.

Carol put the few preliminary statements to one side and studied the photographs closely. They were, as always, grimly distinct. Bryce Darcy lay face down, arms under his body. Close-ups from several angles showed the wounds that had flawed the symmetry of his smooth fair hair. Carol could see what Mark Bourke had meant when he had said it was a neat murder. There was no sign of a struggle, the victim apparently having fallen immediately, without time for any defensive action. It didn't look like a frenzied attack, just a few quick, forceful blows to accomplish an efficient killing.

"Open and shut," Bourke had said, and Carol thought how easy it would be to shrug and let him handle the case himself. But then, she had a niggling feeling that it was all too neat, too predictable. She thought with distaste of the killings she had recently investigated — most of them grim, depressing examples of humanity at its most basic — crimes where motivations were obvious. But this murder seemed different in some way. Perhaps it would end up being just another addition to the sordid list, yet in her mind a welcome curiosity began to uncurl.

CHAPTER TWO

The bright winter sun glared dazzling and hot through the glass, but when Carol wound down the car window the biting westerly wind chilled her face. She sat silent as Constable Newsome drove with admirable precision through heavy traffic to Sydney's northwestern suburb of Baulkham Hills. The Hills District had once been on the edge of Sydney's relentless growth, but was now swallowed up by the inexorable advance of suburbia. Even so, the blocks here were large and market gardens and orchards still survived in some places.

Carol glanced appraisingly at Anne Newsome. She was a high achiever who had topped her class at the Academy and had earned the warm approbation of her superiors in every position she had been given. The young constable had short chestnut curly hair, intelligent brown eyes and smooth olive skin. Of average height and slightly stocky build, she had an air of disciplined enthusiasm, matched by neat, economical movements. She was healthy, fit, and, Carol had noted from her personnel file, a crack shot.

Remembering her conversation in the television channel's make-up room that morning, Carol said, "How difficult do you think it is now for a young woman joining the Force?"

Constable Newsome didn't shift her eyes from the road, but Carol saw the corner of her mouth quirk in an ironic smile. "You mean sexism? Of course it's there. You must know that better than I do. Perhaps things are improving, but sooner or later you run up against the men's club. Then you have to be twice as good as any male before you have a hope."

"You can appeal if you think you've been discriminated against in promotion," said Carol, keeping the sharpness out of her voice, but not out of her thoughts. Surely this young woman had an easy ride, compared to Carol's experiences as a tyro in the Force.

Anne shot a look at her. "Sure, but it can be hard to prove that you're outstanding enough to outrank a man. And often it isn't obvious enough to appeal against. Things just happen — or don't happen. The best thing is to have someone on your side — a mentor, if you like."

13

"And for you that's Mark Bourke?"

Anne shrugged. "Sort of."

Her tone didn't invite further comment, and Carol gazed absently out the window at the clotted traffic, thinking of her own career. *Her* mentor had been the present Commissioner of Police. Some years ago a previous state government had reformed the career opportunities in the Force to reward those with talent, rather than those with professional longevity, and he had risen rapidly through the ranks. Carol's career had had a corresponding ascent, and, although she had earned her promotions, his good offices could not have been a hindrance. Their special relationship still endured, so that she could bypass communication logjams, although this was something she did with care, knowing how easy it would be to build resentment in her colleagues. In turn, the Commissioner relied on Carol's professionalism and the preoccupation the media had with an attractive woman in such a male-dominated area. She got results, she had mastered the ten-second television sound-bite and she was compellingly photogenic — qualities particularly valuable when trenchant criticisms of the police were aired in public.

Anne Newsome broke into her thoughts. "We're almost there."

Carol had intended to discuss the case during the trip, not waste time on fruitless thought. She said briskly, "How did Charlotte Darcy seem to you yesterday?"

After thinking for a moment, Anne said, "To me she looked like she was drugged in some way. I thought it was more than just shock. She was vague and disconnected in the studio, but when I took her into the house to change her clothes she started talking wildly, the words falling over each other. She didn't really make any sense and wasn't responding to any questions I asked. Then the woman psychiatrist came in and took over."

"Was there any blood on her hands?"

"Yes, under the thumbnail of her right hand. Sergeant Bourke asked me to take a swab of it. Some blood on her clothes, too, but nothing else on her skin that I could see."

"Puncture marks?"

Anne shook her head. "If she's injecting drugs she's been careful. Certainly nothing showed on her arms or legs."

Carol realized she hadn't asked Mark Bourke anything about Charlotte Darcy's husband. "What about Eric Higgins? How did he strike you?"

Anne's lips twitched in a slight smile. "Like someone who should have a much grander name. Higgins hardly does him justice."

Amused, Carol said, "What would you suggest?"

"Can't imagine why he didn't adopt his wife's — Darcy has a ring to it, doesn't it — and he certainly thinks he's something special."

The young constable's humorous tone and refusal to treat Carol with over-careful respect was melting Carol's resistance. She found herself interested in what Anne Newsome might say as a person, not just her reaction as an officer present at the scene of a crime. "Did Mr. Higgins seem shaken by what had happened?"

Anne braked to a smooth halt at a red light. Turning to look at Carol, she said, "He didn't take it in his stride, if that's what you mean. He was white, hands trembling, that sort of thing. Even so, I couldn't help noticing he didn't go anywhere near his wife, almost as though he didn't want to be associated with her, and was leaving her on her own to face the music."

Warmed by this unexpected talent for observation in someone she had dismissed as just another inexperienced junior officer, Carol said, "What other impressions did you get . . . just off the top of your head?"

The lights changed to green and Anne accelerated evenly as she considered Carol's question. "Mr. Higgins was very helpful — almost too helpful. But he faded right away when Mr. and Mrs. Darcy turned up. Became the invisible man, maybe because he's intimidated by his father-in-law. There could be some other reason, of course, and I mightn't be fair to him. It's hardly the best circumstance to meet someone for the first time."

As she spoke she was directing the car through open white metal gates and up the smooth curve of a red gravel drive towards a cluster of low-lying white buildings hugging the grassy hill that rose behind them. A great deal of money had been spent on landscaping: lines of Norfolk pines formed windbreaks on two sides of the large block of land, ample flower beds formed terraces of color, and a generous ornamental lake with a small crowd of momentarily flustered ducks provided a barrier between the front security fence and the buildings.

Noticing a gardener digging lethargically, Carol said, "There was a statement from the gardener in the file."

"Yes, Sid Styles. We spoke to him last night. He saw Bryce Darcy arrive here about one o'clock yesterday afternoon, just when he was packing up his gardening tools. Mr. Styles works on the gardens here three mornings a week, usually stopping at midday. He's sure about the time yesterday because he was running later than usual, otherwise he wouldn't have seen Bryce Darcy at all. Says they chatted about the weather for a few moments, then Darcy went inside."

As she was speaking she parked the car in a sandstone forecourt to the house. "Eric Higgins," Anne said as a tall dark-haired man came out to greet them.

"Inspector Ashton," Higgins said in a soft, rich voice as he handed her out of the car. "Of course I've seen you many times on television. How delightful to meet you in person."

However inappropriate his greeting might be, Eric Higgins certainly looked the part of someone under great stress. He was very pale, almost gray, and his expression was strained. His face was a series of straight, uncompromising lines between the angle of his jaw and the rulered edge of his black hair. His eyebrows were firm emphasis to the narrow rectangular blue of his eyes and the aristocratic sculpture of his nose complemented the sensual set of his mouth. He wore well-cut dark slacks, a tan fine-wool sweater and expensive leather casual shoes.

Obviously recognizing Constable Newsome from the night before, he bestowed a slight smile on her, then turned his full attention on Carol. "You're here to see Charlotte's studio, Inspector. It's still sealed, of course."

As he led the way to a separate white building attached to the house by a covered walkway, Carol said, "There are a few things I'd like to go through with you."

"I made a full statement last night." The mild complaint was accented by a slightly theatrical gesture with his open hand.

Carol's response was crisp. "Yes, I've seen that. This is more in the nature of background information."

His cooperative manner evaporated. He stopped and swung around, fixing Carol with a hard blue stare. His voice was still soft, but pulsing with indignation. "What sort of background would you need? It's perfectly obvious what happened. There was an intruder, Bryce disturbed him and was attacked. When Charlotte found her brother's body it was too much for her. She was upset and confused . . . she's not strong. Frankly, Inspector, she hasn't been herself lately."

Conscious of the winter wind's cutting edge, Carol moved forward, forcing Higgins to turn and walk beside her. "Your wife works here alone, does she?" she said pleasantly as Constable Newsome opened white painted double doors.

He said with a touch of weary patience, "Usually. Sometimes in Katoomba. You may know she's the chief designer for the family company. Nora — that's her mother — still does some stuff, but most of it's Charlotte's work."

"Was she using the studio yesterday?"

Higgins moved impatiently. "I've told you — she hasn't been well. Actually, Charlotte hasn't worked much for weeks."

Constable Newsome stood unobtrusively to one side, having opened one side of the double white doors that served as the main entrance to the studio building. Carol paused at the doorway, saying with carefully judged sympathy, "I'm afraid I have to ask these questions, even though it is such a difficult time for you."

Mollified by her tone, Higgins responded as he gestured for her to enter, "It's a nightmare. I can't believe what's happened. Charlotte would be the last person to use violence . . . and she loved Bryce."

Carol nodded assent to his last statement. "So her brother often came here? It wasn't a surprise that he did so yesterday?"

Noting that the question seemed to make Higgins uncomfortable, Carol added, "Was Bryce Darcy a frequent visitor?"

He moved closer to her, his rich voice soft with its implication of a shared confidence. "I've said Charlotte didn't do all her work here. She spent time in the Katoomba studios — that's the original place established by her parents. Bryce was the company accountant and she usually saw him there. He didn't often visit us, especially after . . . well, the friction between them."

His height forced Carol to tilt her head back to maintain eye contact. Resisting the impulse to step back, she said, "Violent arguments have been mentioned."

He was keen to explain. "Yes, but only verbally violent. Certainly not enough to end in murder. Charlotte has been distracted . . . little things would upset her. She's had trouble sleeping, that sort of thing, so she was tired, irritable." He took a breath,

19

and added with a little too much reassurance, "The conflict between them was definitely nothing serious."

Now you've made me suspicious, thought Carol with wry amusement. She asked innocuously, "Were these arguments focused on a particular issue?"

Quick to assure, he said, "No, Inspector, not at all. As I said, Charlotte's been prickly, difficult. Almost anything could upset her in the state she's been in lately."

"Has your wife seen a doctor?"

Higgins looked at her sharply. "As a matter of fact — yes." He added with strong weight, "Not that it has anything to do with this."

Wondering if he was hinting there was something to hide, Carol turned away from him to look around Charlotte Darcy's studio. Skylights let in a stream of diffused light, illuminating a large tilted drawing board bearing the vivid colors of a half-finished design. Workbenches lined the walls. Tools and implements were tidily placed in racks, with larger items stored under the benches. In one corner was a refrigerator, its white enamel door bright with magnetic holders anchoring a variety of pieces of paper. Mugs and materials to make tea or coffee were arranged carefully on a tray and Carol had the fleeting thought that Mark Bourke would heartily approve. A tidy murder, he had called it — was that because he believed his main suspect had an impulse for order?

The floor was warm brown cork tiling, shining clean and marked only by dried blood and the outlines indicating exactly where Bryce Darcy had fallen, and a small bloodstain to one side. A tall work stool stood near where the head of the body had lain.

Catching Carol's glance, Anne Newsome said, "She was sitting on that when the patrol officers came in. The chalk mark shows where the hammer lay on the bench near her."

"Charlotte was in shock, Inspector!" Higgins exclaimed, leaning forward to touch her arm, his soft voice thick with persuasion.

She narrowed her eyes, thinking he would never touch a male officer. She was conscious that Anne Newsome was standing discreetly to one side, alert to the nuances of the combat.

Higgins apparently sensed Carol's hostility. He removed his fingers as he said, "Actually, my wife *was* seeing a psychiatrist. Nothing serious, of course, just stress."

"She was a patient of Dr. Naomi Reed's?"

The question seemed to irritate him. "No. Dr. Reed was brought in by my father-in-law. Keith collected her on the way here after I'd called and said what had happened."

Carol began to move around the studio, checking sight lines from the doorway to see at which point a body would have been seen. He followed her, saying, "Is that all, Inspector?"

She said, "Mr. Keith Darcy didn't come all the way from Katoomba, did he?"

"No. He and Nora were at their city apartment near Hyde Park." He sighed, lifting his shoulders and extending his hands palms up. "It was a dreadful situation. I didn't know what to do. I rang Keith and Nora, called the police, and just waited . . ."

Carol's voice held polite inquiry. "And you didn't think it would be better to move your wife away from her brother's body?"

"She was in a daze — she didn't know where she was." He became belligerent. "Anyway, what difference does it make?"

What a tempting tableau it made, Carol thought. The victim at the killer's feet. She said, "Do you know if your wife had been taking any type of drug? For example, tranquilizers or painkillers of any kind?"

He shook his head. "No, nothing. At least . . ."

It was obvious he expected Carol to prompt him to continue, so she said, "At least what?"

"As I said, Charlotte's been very nervy lately. I never thought of drugs, but now that you mention it . . ."

Don't take up a career in acting, Carol thought, keeping an expression of neutral interest on her face.

Almost as though he knew what she was thinking, he said with deep conviction, "Look, Inspector, Charlotte couldn't kill anyone, even Bryce at his worst. I can't believe she's been taking any drugs, she's just been under a lot of strain lately. On top of that, the shock of finding the body . . ."

"You came into your wife's studio as soon as you arrived home?"

Her matter-of-factness seemed to disturb him. He said defensively, "Look, I've been through this before. I was visiting my video outlets, found I needed some business papers, called back here at approximately three-thirty, saw Bryce's car, knew he'd be with Charlotte, so came into the studio to find her sitting looking at his body."

"Exactly where was she when you found her?"

"It's in my statement! Do I have to go over it again and again?" His response to Carol's silence was petulant. "Oh, all right! She was on that work stool over there. It hasn't been moved, that's just where it was. And she was staring at Bryce as though it was something amazing, something she couldn't really understand. I spoke to her, but she didn't seem to hear me. I knelt, looked at Bryce's head, realized there was nothing I could do. I went to the phone — it's next to the refrigerator — and called my in-laws, then the police."

Carol had read his statement and knew he was repeating it almost word for word. She said, "Your wife didn't speak to you during this whole time?"

He shook his head. "Not a word. She didn't seem to know where she was." He slid his sleeve up to consult his watch, a slim gold Rolex. "Inspector, if there's nothing else, I'm afraid I must make some important phone calls."

Carol smiled pleasantly. "There will be some other questions later, but I have just two more things I'd like to ask you about."

Higgins allowed himself the luxury of letting his impatience show. "Yes?" he said shortly.

"Firstly, what did *you* think of your brother-in-law?"

His handsome face blank, Higgins said, "We weren't close friends, if that's what you mean. We didn't have any interests in common. If you want my frank opinion, Bryce was rather boring. You know the sort — a typical accountant, gray and conservative." He added, as though it was a clinching argument, "He drove a Volvo." Putting his hands in his pockets in what seemed to be a deliberate attempt to seem at ease, he continued, "And what's your other question?"

"I'd like the name of the psychiatrist your wife saw and, if you're willing to give it, a general idea of his or her diagnosis of your wife's condition."

He responded with an alacrity that made Carol sure he'd been waiting for the opportunity. "Dr. George Fillington. Actually, he's a friend, as well as a doctor. I know him through the local Lions Club. As for George's diagnosis . . ." After a pause to shake his head regretfully, he went on, "I don't know if you realize Charlotte had a child when she was sixteen. Her name's Megan and she's twenty-four now. Charlotte turns forty-one this year. When we married six years ago we both hoped to have a family. Unfortunately, that wasn't to be . . ."

His next pause, Carol felt, was to survey the effect of his words. Carol knew she looked sympathetic: Anne Newsome, notebook open, was attentive. Summoning a rueful smile Higgins went on, "It's the biological clock of course, ticking away. George says Charlotte's depressed at her failure to conceive, guilty about what happened when she was a kid, and then, add pressure of work — it was all too much for her."

Sure that he was waiting for a comment to indicate an empathetic response, Carol said without a trace of irony, "Mr. Higgins, I'd like to thank you for your patience and cooperation."

Effectively dismissed, he frowned, then, with forced graciousness he excused himself and left them.

Watching the stiff line of his broad shoulders as he retreated, Carol said to Anne Newsome, "How does he compare to yesterday when you saw him?"

Anne tilted her head as she considered the question. "He's obviously gained self-possession. Yesterday he looked sick and frightened."

"Frightened? Not just shocked?"

Anne was decisive. "No. I got the impression he was scared of something, but I don't think it was just the possibility his wife might be arrested for murder."

"What do we know of his background?"

"Not much, yet. Ralph Ferguson's checking on it. He runs a small chain of video rental outlets called Eric's Magic Video. There's some suggestion he's in a bit of financial trouble, but if that's true no doubt his wife could bail him out with some of her Darcy Designs money."

Carol said, "What's your general impression of Eric Higgins, now that you've seen him twice?"

"I don't think he's very bright," she said dismissively. She added with a grin, "Good-looking though, which is better than nothing."

* * * * *

Home uncharacteristically early, Carol was greeted with feline enthusiasm by Sinker and Jeffrey, but not by Sybil. She had expected her to be there and was surprised by her resentment when she read the note on the kitchen bench: *Carol — If you beat me home, I'm with Vicki. See you soon.*

The cats were delighted to be inside, as the winter westerly swooping across the gray-green of the harbor had a cold sting. Carol stood behind the protection of plate glass and watched the spectacular sunset. The wind had heaped huge piles of clouds in artistic clumps, allowing the sun to spear through with yellow shafts of Biblical light which were theatrically reflected in the ruffled waters of Middle Harbour.

The beautiful expanse of sky, harbor and bushland had often soothed Carol. Today almost everything seemed to have the ability to excite her impatience or anger. She turned abruptly away from nature to survey the comforts of her house.

Polished wooden floors flooded with light from the huge plate glass windows, bright rugs, stylish modern pale wood furniture, her battered old coffee percolator perched on the edge of the breakfast bar . . . familiar objects, yet somehow unsatisfying. Carol was suddenly filled with the desire to be somewhere else — to be someone else.

She was angry at her irritability. She was successful in her career, was in a long-term relationship with Sybil, had every reason to be content.

The sound of the front door opening broke into her thoughts. When Sybil came laughing into the room, curly red hair wild from the wind, Carol said what she hadn't meant to say, "Where the hell have you been?"

"Didn't you see my note?"

Somehow Sybil's hug and kiss were an added burden, as was her uncomplicated cheerfulness. Carol felt ridiculously sullen as Sybil described the women's meeting she had just attended. She didn't want to hear about Vicki Thorpe's dynamic approach to women's rights.

"Vicki's coming over to our side of the harbor to see a woman doctor who's been involved in treating and counseling victims of domestic violence. Then Vicki's going to drop off any material she gets from the doctor for me to use in our submission."

Carol's tone was wary. "Submission?"

"For an expanded women's refuge program for the inner city. Actually, Vicki was wondering if you'd like to help." Grinning at Carol's mild astonishment, Sybil continued, "By providing some local statistics on domestic violence, Carol, such as successful prosecutions and the effectiveness of restraining orders. That's all — Vicki certainly isn't going to ask you to patrol the barricades."

"Good thing, too," said Carol with a reluctant smile.

The problem, Carol thought, was that Vicki Thorpe was so dynamic, so unadornedly enthusiastic about any project that had positive advantages for women, that it seemed churlish to deny her when she made a request. Added to this was a personal agreeableness, more fundamental than mere charm, that almost made cooperation and support for Vicki's campaigns a pleasant duty.

Even before she had met her, Carol had been familiar with Vicki Thorpe's history. Vicki's husband, a well-known journalist, had facilitated her access to influential people and assisted her in building a high public profile. This continuous publicity had not always been favorable. The Family First movement, in particular, had targeted her support for abortion on demand, her position on a media council concerned with AIDS education, and her excursions into the sanctity of the home in the guise of a campaigner against domestic violence, as symptomatic of a pervasive moral sickness.

In the past, whenever Vicki Thorpe hit the news, Carol had regarded her with abstract approval — her stance on women's issues was the one Carol told herself *she* would have taken, had she not been constrained by her position in the police force. But this positive view of Vicki Thorpe had changed somewhat when Sybil met her in person.

As a teacher, Sybil had become involved in the provision of free basic English classes for migrant women, a group in society often exploited by clothing manufacturers as a cheap, non-unionized source of piecework labor. Hampered by poor English skills, many migrant women spent long hours each day sewing garments in their homes for a few cents for each item. Vicki's crusade against these practices had as its key step education, and this brought her to adult basic education as run by TAFE colleges. Sybil, who was teaching a related course — Literacy Volunteer Tutoring — had been an immediate convert to Vicki's political activism on this particular issue, and from this followed opportunities to enter a wider range of women's concerns.

Carol had been supportive, of course. Sybil's interests, once so narrow, now encompassed, Carol privately thought, rather too wide a field. And when Sybil first introduced her to Vicki Thorpe, Carol had been keen to meet the woman who was the catalyst for such a change.

She could still remember how disconcerted she had been by Vicki's first question, "Would you call yourself a feminist?"

She was still uncomfortable remembering her reply, "I suppose so — I have to admit I haven't thought about it very deeply."

To be honest with herself, Carol had to admit that some of the resentment she felt towards Vicki Thorpe was based on that one telling question. And, of course, there was Sybil's increasing interest in women's issues, an interest that took much of the precious time that Carol had become accustomed to spending with her.

Later that evening, before Vicki arrived, Sybil said, her face serious, "Carol, do you mind Vicki coming here? Tell me if you do."

"Have I said anything to make you think that?"

Sybil smiled at Carol's evasion. "Come on, answer the question."

Carol shrugged. "Darling, it's just that I always feel besieged by her — she always wants something . . ."

Looking at her speculatively, Sybil said, "And that's your honest reply? There isn't any more to it?

Carol said lightly, "I'm not jealous, if that's what you mean."

Before Sybil could respond, a series of authoritative knocks vibrated the front door. "That's got to be Vicki," said Carol drily.

When Vicki, radiating tireless enthusiasm, followed Sybil into the living room, Carol tried to evaluate her objectively. She was below average

29

height, slightly built, with long, straight brown hair tied back in a careless ponytail. Irritatingly she was one of those people who could wear the most casual and undistinguished clothes with élan. Her large brown eyes were her best physical feature, although her slightly hooked, strong nose gave strength and purpose to her face. She spoke quickly, alert and concentrated in all she said. She was not accustomed to wasting time with small talk and would impatiently brush away chat about inconsequential matters.

She was also charmingly ruthless about tapping into others' skills and areas of expertise. It was typical that Vicki should come with several tasks for Carol to accomplish, taking it for granted that she would comply. "It will be so much help, Carol, when you provide the details on domestic violence I've noted here for you."

"Vicki, I can't promise . . ."

"Of course you can't. I appreciate how busy you are. It will be so valuable to have hard data, though."

Carol left Vicki and Sybil planning the campaign and went to prime her ancient coffee percolator. She sighed as she glanced down the list of items Vicki expected her to research. After all, how in all conscience could she refuse to help other women in situations of discomfort, unhappiness and danger she had never had to endure? And even more than Vicki Thorpe she had seen the violent end results of family conflict. To do something positive to prevent or lessen the terror in which some women and children lived each day . . .

She smiled grimly as she put the list into her briefcase. Vicki Thorpe, she thought, you're even getting to *me*.

CHAPTER THREE

From the street, Carol thought, the Naomi Reed Clinic looked like a palatial northern suburbs mansion. Artful landscaping hid the substantial car park behind glossy leaves of flowering shrubs, and the main entrance, where she waited with Bourke while Constable Newsome parked the car, was dominated by a fountain constructed of metal whorls over which the water ran down in hypnotic spiral patterns. The clinic itself had an impressive sandstone façade and was set in beautiful gardens, presenting, at a price, soothing vistas to troubled minds.

Carol had met Dr. Naomi Reed once before, and wondered if she would remember the occasion. The doctor, a renowned specialist in mental illness, particularly schizophrenia and depression, was generally known to the public because of her services to the moneyed end of the market and her willingness to engage in subtle self-promotion as a resident expert on radio and television.

The indulged children of the rich entered her clinic to be weaned off their dependencies, wives who had dulled their days with tranquilizers could book in for a short break from home duties, and those for whom the pressures of business had become too much could dry out discreetly and comfortably.

Dr. Reed greeted Carol and Mark Bourke with a restrained smile and outstretched hand, as they entered her sumptuous office. Anne Newsome, who stood politely behind her superior officers, she ignored. She spoke rapidly, yet each word was pronounced with careful precision. "Inspector Ashton! I'm delighted to see you. We shared a program once, you may recall."

Carol smiled politely, remembering the hum of activity in the television studio that had surrounded this diminutive woman's crackling energy. "I believe you've already met Detective Sergeant Bourke and Detective Constable Newsome."

Naomi Reed shook Bourke's hand briefly, then gestured for her visitors to seat themselves on thickly upholstered peach-colored chairs a slightly darker shade than the pastel walls. "Yes," she said,

"I met Sergeant Bourke briefly the night before last. Poor Bryce."

Her tone of regret caused Bourke to say in mild surprise, "I didn't realize you knew Bryce Darcy well."

"I would count myself as a friend of his parents, Keith and Nora. I've known them for some time. Regarding Bryce, I feel I should mention that he did informally consult me about his sister."

Carol glanced at Bourke to indicate he should continue to run the interview, then she sat back to assess the doctor's responses. Carol thought many patients would draw comfort from that air of alert superiority. Seated at ease behind the protection of her large blond wood desk, Naomi Reed wore a crisply white, tailored medical coat with understated style, complementing its professional lines with discreet gold jewelry. Her graying hair was swept back in a smooth chignon, her sharp features softened with expertly applied make-up. Her dark eyes watched Bourke intently as he asked why Bryce Darcy had consulted her about his sister.

Her reply was delivered with concise precision. "As Charlotte Darcy's doctor, I am constrained as to what I can tell you without her permission or that of her father."

Bourke reacted immediately. "Her father? Does that mean she's not competent to speak for herself? Has her husband been consulted on the matter?" When Dr. Reed didn't respond to his questions, he said, "Are we able to interview her?"

Naomi Reed steepled her fingers and looked reflectively at Anne Newsome, who was unobtrusively writing in her notebook. "Charlotte cannot be interviewed today. However, I have discussed matters with both Charlotte and her parents, and her husband, of course, and have been empowered to give you certain information."

Realizing that Dr. Reed was accustomed to controlling interviews, Carol decided to disturb the balance. She said bluntly, "Of course we respect doctor–patient relationships, but as this is a murder investigation we must insist on your full cooperation."

A look of mild surprise enhanced the doctor's polite protest. "And you have my full cooperation, Inspector."

"Then as Bryce Darcy made what you called an informal approach to you about his sister, there can be no objection in telling about his concerns."

In response to Carol's definitive statement, Naomi Reed leaned back, pursing her lips thoughtfully. After a moment she said, "In essence, Bryce thought his sister's behavior was becoming increasingly erratic. He was worried that she might be on the verge of a breakdown. He said he'd spoken to Eric, Charlotte's husband, but had been told to mind his own business. His concern was such that he came to me for advice."

"Which was?" prompted Bourke.

Naomi Reed lifted her shoulders in a slight shrug. "Which was that I could do nothing unless Charlotte came to me as a patient. Based on Bryce's descriptions of her behavior, his sister did seem to be under some stress, and I suggested that he encourage her to see a doctor. I, of course, would have been happy to have her consult me, but I heard nothing further. And that was where the matter rested until the day before yesterday. Charlotte Darcy *is* my patient now, and, as I said, I do have certain information that I have been instructed to give you."

Bourke wanted further clarification. "Is this to do with the fact she isn't available for interview?"

Dr. Reed's tone was crisp. "Yes. As standard practice, when Charlotte came here on Monday I ran a series of tests. Urine analysis showed she had recently ingested a considerable dose of amphetamines, within the last two days. As you may know, at this point her body will have excreted only about thirty percent of the drug, so I cannot allow her to be subjected to questioning yet."

Bourke said quickly, "It's your medical opinion Charlotte Darcy took a large dose of amphetamines the day her brother died."

"I didn't say that, Sergeant. My point is that it's possible my patient has ingested amphetamines within the last forty-eight hours. That's as far as I'm willing to go on the evidence available. With Mrs. Darcy's permission, I'd be happy to provide the results of the blood and urine tests for your examination."

Bourke was persistent. "Was Mrs. Darcy's behavior when you saw her on Monday afternoon consistent with someone who had recently taken amphetamines — say that morning?"

Her professional demeanor was disturbed by an irritated frown. She said peremptorily, "Possibly. That's all I'll say."

Carol interposed, "Do you see this as a one-time use, or something more regular?"

Dr. Reed's pause indicated her reluctance to

answer. She finally said, "I think we may be looking at long-term use of amphetamines in this case. There may well have been a constant high dosage for a period of months."

"Any evidence of needle marks?"

"None," said Dr. Reed with a trace of impatience.

At a glance from Carol, Bourke took up the questioning again. "Would amphetamine abuse explain her erratic behavior over the last few months?"

Dr. Reed nodded her neat head in agreement. "Very possibly."

"Could you comment on the form the drugs might take? Could they have been legally prescribed by her doctor?"

Naomi Reed said tartly, "I should think that highly unlikely. Stimulants such as amphetamines can be administered for certain medical conditions, for example narcolepsy where patients have a constant irresistible tendency to fall asleep. They are also sometimes used as appetite suppressants for the severely obese. Neither situation applies here."

"Could you offer any explanation as to where she might have obtained the drug?"

"That's your area of expertise, Sergeant. I can only tell you the medical side. In my opinion, Charlotte Darcy has been suffering the effects of large doses of amphetamines for some time. This would explain her emotional fluctuations and her altered thinking patterns. She is now suffering withdrawal symptoms, including severe depression."

Leaning forward, Bourke said, "Could she have become irrational enough to murder her brother?"

"I'm not in a position to make any comment,

Sergeant." She dismissed him by turning her attention to Carol. "You will be anxious to interview Charlotte, Inspector. She will be staying here in the clinic to allow me to monitor her recovery. Naturally, if you wish an independent medical assessment of her condition I will cooperate fully."

Carol smiled. "I'm sure it isn't necessary, but as a matter of form we'll arrange for an additional medical examination immediately."

Naomi Reed signaled that she considered their conversation was ending by closing the file in front of her and aligning her silver pen precisely parallel with its edge. She said, "I believe you will be able to interview her yourself by Friday, perhaps earlier, depending on her progress."

"I do have one other question. I'd like your comments on the choice of amphetamines. Isn't it true that the most common drugs of abuse for women like Charlotte Darcy would be tranquilizers or alcohol?"

"Indeed, that's correct. This is possibly because both are readily available from legal sources."

Carol persisted. "You're not surprised at the use of amphetamines in this case?"

The doctor permitted herself a wintry smile. "Nothing surprises me, Inspector." Rising from her chair she added, "I have patients waiting, so I must leave you, but Keith and Nora Darcy have been staying in the suite we have for relatives, and have asked if they might see you."

Bourke was unwilling to let her escape so easily. "Dr. Reed, might we trouble you for one more thing . . . Would you mind detailing the physical and psychological effects of this type of amphetamine abuse for Constable Newsome? It would be of great help to us."

Naomi Reed inclined her head in reluctant assent as she pressed a button to summon her secretary. Carol said, "I wonder, Dr. Reed, if I could have your personal, rather than your professional, opinion of Bryce Darcy. What we're looking for is an overall impression of his personality and how he related to others."

Naomi Reed's expression softened. "There are too few people like Bryce, Inspector. He was rather shy, cautious, gentle in the best sense of the word. His concern about his sister was absolutely genuine."

"Is there any suggestion that it wasn't?" asked Carol, surprised.

The doctor's smile was cynical. "I believe Charlotte's husband was of the opinion that the family was worried about her because she was the principal creative force behind Darcy Designs, the implication being that their anxiety was spurred by financial, rather than personal, concerns." She broke off as her secretary entered. "Dawn, please take Inspector Ashton and Sergeant Bourke to the guest suite and arrange for refreshments."

Carol had expected the suite to be luxurious, but was still surprised by its opulence. A thick pale gray carpet lapped cream walls hung with original Australian paintings, mainly restful landscapes. French windows framed by heavy full-length salmon pink drapes opened out onto a balcony overlooking the disciplined green of lawns and garden. The furniture was sleekly dark, shining with a patina of expensive good taste.

Carol recognized two of the three people waiting

for them in the suite. Keith and Nora Darcy she knew through her Aunt Sarah. The third, a dark-haired young woman in casual clothes, seated by the French windows, glanced around as Carol and Bourke entered, then looked pointedly back to the view of the garden.

Keith Darcy had changed little since Carol had last seen him at her Aunt Sarah's house. He had a bulky, imposing presence, with thick shoulders and a flat-footed, confident stance. His face was rectangular, deeply tanned and marked with determined lines emphasized by his heavy eyebrows and thick mustache. His hair, streaked with gray, was cut short and brushed back with no attempt at styling. He wore a dark suit, white shirt, and the tie of an exclusive club.

That morning Mark Bourke had filled in the details about him that Carol had not known, or had forgotten. About twenty years ago Keith Darcy had taken over the moderately successful family company, Darcy Designs, when his elder brother, Walter, died. Using his entrepreneurial skills and the creative talents of his wife, Nora, he had built the concern into a spectacular marketing enterprise, first capturing a large slice of the domestic market with Darcy Designs' distinctive range of decor items, furnishings, and up-market T-shirts, wrapping papers and cards. Having consolidated the Australian market, he had then turned his attention overseas. His export drive had been so effective that he had recently been honored with an Order of Australia for his services to export sales. Mark Bourke had added rather cynically, "And, Carol, Darcy made sure he was in the running for an award by getting himself involved with charities helping underprivileged youth. Twang a heartstring and make money for your country — how could you miss public recognition?"

Her thoughts were interrupted as Keith Darcy took both her hands, his manner suggesting a close friendship between them that, as far as Carol was concerned, did not exist. His usually booming voice subdued, he said, "Carol, I'm so glad you're handling this matter."

"Actually, Detective Bourke has the main responsibility for the case. You've met, I know."

As the two men shook hands, Carol could tell from Mark Bourke's slight wince that Keith was employing his usual crushing grip.

Keith Darcy introduced his wife and his granddaughter Megan. Lighting a cigarette with jerky movements, Megan Darcy barely acknowledged the introduction, while Nora Darcy stood silently to one side, hardly seeming part of the scene. She looked distant, unfocused, her graying blonde hair escaping in wisps from tortoise shell clasps at each side of her head, the lines of her face slack. Although she was a big woman, well matched to her husband's bulk, she gave the impression of being somehow insubstantial. Carol, knowing what a talented designer she was, wondered why she had chosen such an unbecoming shade of purple to wear. She said, "Mrs. Darcy, I'm so sorry to meet you again in such circumstances."

Her attention caught, Nora Darcy became more animated, locking glances with Carol with something almost like defiance in her eyes. "You're not going to arrest Charlotte, are you?"

It was a question Carol couldn't answer. She

said, "It would help us if you could tell us all you know."

Keith was frowning. "We know Charlotte isn't well, and Naomi must have told you she thinks it's drugs — amphetamines."

"Speed," added Nora, surprisingly.

Her grandmother's contribution to the conversation seemed to infuse Megan with energy. She viciously stubbed out her cigarette and stalked over to join them. As Keith gestured for everyone to seat themselves on the fatly plush armchairs or couch there was a knock at the door and a uniformed maid entered with a tray heavy with a silver tea service and coffee pots, bone china cups and a selection of continental pastries. Nora Darcy brightened at a familiar task, determining preferences and dispensing cups efficiently, apparently oblivious to the series of pointed questions Bourke was asking her husband.

Despite a mild look of protest from her grandmother, Megan lit another cigarette. She gazed steadfastly at Mark Bourke as she sucked smoke into her lungs as though deprived of nicotine for some time. Carol studied her, noting the stains from smoking on her fingers, and the tight, nervous movements of her hands. Megan Darcy was thin, intense, brooding, almost, Carol thought, as though she had decided to embody the stereotype of angst. Sensing she was being watched, Megan swung her dark glance to meet Carol's eyes. A challenge was given by her cold stare, one that faltered at Carol's faint, sympathetic smile. She frowned and looked away.

Bourke's questions had angered Keith Darcy. The

volume of his voice rose as he stated that his daughter would not voluntarily take any drugs, not even those prescribed by a doctor. She had inherited her mother's artistic talents and temperament, being inclined to mood swings at the best of times, he declared, so it was some time before he had thought anything was wrong, although he was sure, looking back on things, that his daughter had been behaving erratically for some months.

Unmoved by his anger, Bourke said, "What do you mean by erratic?"

"Her emotions seemed so intense, and they'd change abruptly. One minute Charlotte would be on top of the world, having seized on some wonderful new idea that she'd be wildly enthusiastic about — then she'd become irritable, depressed, unable to work. She does quite a lot of her preliminary designs in our factory in the Blue Mountains where we have the staff to run with her ideas. A couple of times recently I found her there early in the morning because she'd been up all night working on something."

When Bourke asked if Charlotte had discussed any problems with either of them, Nora interrupted her husband's strong denials. "She loves Keith, but she wouldn't talk about personal matters with him. She *did* say something to me."

Keith Darcy looked both angry and hurt. "I'm her father. She can say anything to me — anything."

Patting his hand to both placate and silence him, Nora said, "Charlotte asked me if I thought she was going mad, because she couldn't understand it herself, you see. What frightened her was the feeling wonderful, full of energy, and then falling all the way to the bottom. And then she thought her memory was going — she got confused, forgot things . . ."

In the silence that followed Nora's words Megan mashed a cigarette butt to shreds in an ashtray and Keith held his wife's hand tightly, though whether it was for comfort or as a warning to say no more, Carol couldn't decide. She said briskly, "Her husband Eric arranged for her to see a psychiatrist, didn't he?"

"A psychiatrist, yes, but not Naomi Reed!" exclaimed Keith Darcy, making it clear he thought this an important point. There was a sneer in his voice as he went on, "No one with a decent reputation, just a *friend* of Eric's from one of those little clubs he belongs to. Some suburban quack."

"You didn't approve?" said Bourke, deadpan.

Darcy shrugged his heavy shoulders. "I only go for the best." He turned impatiently to Carol. "Look, Charlotte's been fed these things. She wouldn't take them herself. It's impossible."

Aware of how many relatives were astonished and disbelieving, even when faced with overwhelming evidence that a family member was abusing drugs, Carol knew his firm statement might well be wishful thinking. To change the subject, she said, "Bryce's wife, Wilma — have you seen her?"

Darcy said tonelessly, "Wilma's at her sister's place at Parramatta. She's brought the boys down with her."

Bourke said, "We did ask Mrs. Darcy to contact us if she was leaving the Blue Mountains area. The local police there have spoken to her but we haven't interviewed her yet. We were told she was too upset."

With a hint of contempt, Darcy said, "Oh, she's dropped her bundle, all right."

"Keith, she was distraught . . ."

"Come on, there was trouble in that marriage," he said bluntly. He turned his attention to Carol. "Bryce is . . . was our accountant. Bloody good at it too. Wilma worked in the office, a pretty little thing. Set her cap on Bryce, and, by God, she got him. They've been married, what, six, seven years? Two little boys — bonzer little blokes. But Wilma was getting restless. Didn't want to stay in the Blue Mountains, wanted to move down to Sydney."

Nora interposed with more authority than Carol expected. "Keith, be fair. Wilma and Bryce wanted the boys to go to Bryce's old school, and that meant that when they were old enough they'd have to take the train from Katoomba to Sydney and back again every day. I agree with Wilma — it's too much to expect children to spend all that time traveling, and she wouldn't put them in boarding school, which was the only alternative."

"Bryce boarded," snapped Keith. "It didn't hurt him." There was a pause, and Carol suddenly realized that his mouth was trembling and his eyes had filled with tears.

Compassion made her voice gentle. "I'm sorry to keep on asking questions, but that's the only way we can find out what happened." To Nora she said, "Do you think there was a serious difference between your son and his wife?"

Nora moved her hands ineffectually. "Something

wasn't right, but Bryce wasn't one to share things with his family. Always been quiet, thoughtful. Kept his real feelings hidden. He was thirty-five when he married Wilma. As you see, he didn't rush into things. And it seemed a good marriage . . . at least I would have said so until the last few months." She rubbed her brow, her shoulders sagging. "Perhaps it's my fault — if only I'd *made* him tell me what was wrong . . ."

There was a faint derisive sound from Megan. Carol looked at her questioningly, but received only a blank stare in response. Carol said, "Is there anything you'd like to add, Ms Darcy?"

"Not at the moment, thank you." The words were civil, but the tone bellicose. Carol noticed how unsuitable the light, clear timbre of Megan's voice was to the sullen impression her manner created.

Bourke asked several more questions of Keith Darcy, established the family's whereabouts for the rest of the week and promised to advise them if any important developments occurred. As Carol and Bourke rose to go, Megan said abruptly, "I'm leaving too. I'll walk down with you."

As the three of them came out into the glare of winter sunlight, she turned. "Look, I know it looks bad for my mother." She spoke with jerky urgency. "What I'm asking is, don't take the easy path, okay? You can pin it on her, I know you can. I just don't want that bastard she's married to getting away with it. My mother didn't kill Uncle Bryce. I can't prove it, but I'm bloody sure Eric did it."

Carol said, "Why?"

Megan's dark eyes narrowed in disdain. "Eric's been bleeding Mum for years. He fancies himself a crash-hot businessman — runs a video business he says is successful, but I happen to know it's about to go belly-up. Uncle Bryce was an accountant and he knew what was happening but Mum wouldn't listen."

Thinking of Eric Higgins' firm assertion that the conflict between Charlotte and her brother had no particular focus, Carol said, "Your mother and your uncle argued violently about Eric?"

"Yes, but she didn't want to know the truth."

Bourke said, "If your mother wouldn't take her brother's advice, where's the motive? How was Bryce a threat to your stepfather?"

Megan smiled coldly. "Oh, he was a threat all right. You see, Uncle Bryce told me just last week that he was going to cut off the money. Said he'd stop the monthly payment from Darcy Designs to my mother's account. Said he knew Eric couldn't last long without funds — said his creditors would pull him under."

CHAPTER FOUR

That afternoon when Carol returned to her office from a meeting called by Superintendent Edgar — an affable man, but one relentlessly attuned to any political influences that might enhance his career — she found Mark Bourke waiting for her.

"Surprise," she said to him, "Keith Darcy and the Minister for Police went to school together. I've just been told, indirectly of course, that this case should be handled discreetly."

She didn't add the bitter thought that in effect

she'd just been patted on the head and told to be a good girl and not rock the boat.

Bourke was looking pleased with himself. "Well, the facts are mounting up, so I don't think we're far from an arrest, and I don't see how we can be discreet about that, unless we wait until something even more interesting hits the news."

His buoyant tone brought a wry smile to Carol's lips as she seated herself behind her desk. "Am I to take it the facts don't look good for Charlotte Darcy?"

"We haven't found any trace of amphetamines in the house or in the studio. What we have got is a positive on blood. The blood on her clothes matches her brother's group," he said, handing her with a flourish close-up photographs of a pair of jeans and a long-sleeved shirt. "I direct your attention to the smears on the jeans and the blood-soaked cuff on the shirt."

Carol studied the photographs closely. "No spray of droplets? With that type of blow it could be a possibility."

"Well, you can't have everything, Carol. There was matching blood under her right thumbnail, but any other blood on her hands she wiped off on her jeans, hence the smears on the thighs. The hammer handle is covered with a rough surface to give a good grip, so it was no go for fingerprints, but there's a fine set of her prints higher up on the metal shaft."

"Hardly surprising, since it happens to be her hammer in the first place."

Ignoring her dry comment, he pointed to the

close-up photographs. "You can clearly see where blood's soaked into the cuff of the right-hand sleeve."

"No doubt, along with the majority of the population, she's right-handed?"

"She is. The pathologist says Bryce was hit once from behind when he was upright, then to finish him off, a second blow when he had fallen. That's the point where I think Charlotte got blood on her sleeve, when she was making sure she'd done a good job."

"And what are your other facts?" said Carol with an ironic emphasis on the last word.

"He died between two and three on Monday afternoon, with the best bet close to two-thirty. It's almost certain he wouldn't have known what hit him. The first blow from the hammer cracked his skull."

Absently, Carol began to twist her black opal ring. She felt provoked, first by the Superintendent's bland expectation that she would make sure any publicity for the case would be stifled — and now, by Bourke's certainty that Charlotte Darcy was guilty. She said, "And your chief suspect is strong enough to hit her brother that hard?"

Bourke ducked his head in conviction. "Absolutely. This particular hammer's a lovely tool, well-balanced and made to concentrate the energy of a blow into a small area. All she'd need is a good swing and a murderous intent."

"There was a small blood stain on the floor near the body . . ."

Bourke smiled at her deliberately off-hand tone. "You'll be pleased to know I even have an explanation for that, Carol. Charlotte hits him once, he falls, so she puts the hammer down while she investigates how successful she's been. He's still breathing, so she picks it up, has another go, then perches herself on the work stool with the hammer placed lovingly beside her on the bench."

"How convenient," said Carol caustically, "that Charlotte Darcy's brainstorms are interspersed with periods when she acts with cool precision."

He spread his hands. "When she's in a state of amphetamine intoxication, who can predict what she might do from one minute to the next?"

Carol said, "What if she saw someone else murder him, but didn't understand what was happening?"

"Haven't ruled anything out, Carol." His tone indicated he wanted to reassure her. "I'm going through Bryce's personal effects at the moment. Who knows — maybe there's someone out there with a stunning motive we know nothing about."

"What about his will?"

"Well, he certainly has money, thanks to the success of Darcy Designs, which is run as a partnership with each member having an equal share. Apart from that, Bryce Darcy had a wide range of prudent investments, so he's worth a lot. Most of it goes to his wife and two sons — and the rest of his family's well off anyway."

"So there's nothing unusual about it?"

Bourke scratched his chin. "No. He did leave money to a couple of societies in the Blue Mountains, one historical and the other concerned with conservation. Just in the last few months he added a codicil to the will leaving several original paintings to a nephew and two nieces who live in Brisbane."

This caught Carol's interest. "Valuable paintings?"

Bourke shrugged. "Don't know. *I* didn't recognize the artists, but that doesn't mean much. I'll check it out, if you like."

As he rose to go, Carol said, "Mark, would you close the door . . . I'd like to speak to you about something else."

He immediately sobered, obeying her instruction and then returning to his chair. After a pause, during which Carol tried to formulate her words, he said urgently, "Carol, you're not going to resign, are you?"

Astonished, she stared at him. "Why would you think that?"

He moved his hands in an aimless gesture. "Sorry, I spoke out of turn. Forget I said anything."

She wanted to lighten the awkwardness between them, but could think of nothing to say.

He was running his hand across the short stubble of his hair, his face flushed. "Carol, I shouldn't have said anything. It's just that you've seemed . . . well . . . unhappy lately. With your job, I mean. At least, that's the impression I've got . . ." His voice trailed away.

Feeling a matching embarrassment, Carol said rapidly, "Look, Mark, it's my turn to be sorry. I was going to ask you about Anne Newsome, and now I wish I'd never even thought of it."

He was obviously puzzled. "About Anne?"

Carol sighed. "I have to say it now, I suppose.

It's about your relationship with her. I was wondering if there's anything personal there."

Bourke grinned. "I'm flattered you'd think Anne might lust after me, Carol. Unfortunately, she seems quite impervious to my charms." He added quickly, "And I'm not the slightest interested in her that way. I want to help her because she's going to be a bloody good officer." He looked down at his hands. "Actually, Carol, lately I've been going out with someone."

His comment invited a personal response, and Carol, wanting to find a way to drop the subject of Anne Newsome, said, "Is it serious?"

"Could be."

Carol realized this most mundane of interactions was making her feel uncomfortable because she was unwilling to be as open and direct as Bourke appeared ready to be. Usually so single-mindedly professional, he was sharing something of his private life with her, and, despite her misgivings, she found herself wanting to show him she appreciated what he was doing. She said, "Anyone I know?"

"I've mentioned her — Patricia James. She works at the Art Gallery." He seemed to be growing more uneasy by the moment and Carol felt as anxious as he to end their conversation. She felt a ridiculous impulse to say she was sorry again. Instead she said, "Would you give me a copy of the autopsy and the forensic reports?"

He immediately stood, visibly relieved at the return to business. "Sure. And Anne can give you a report on Dr. George Fillington, the psychiatrist Eric Higgins sent his wife to see."

His sardonic tone sparked Carol's interest. "Something there?"

"Let's just say I think only a woman could do the good doctor justice, so I'll send Constable Newsome in to tell you all about it."

Anne Newsome appeared at Carol's door half an hour later. "Inspector? You wanted to see me?"

"Mark says your comments on the interview with Dr. Fillington would be of particular value."

"I may be biased," said Anne, smiling slightly.

As she described the interview, Carol's initial aversion to Eric Higgins' smooth persona hardened into dislike. Although his wife's behavior had surely indicated the possibility of serious mental or emotional disturbance, he had taken her to see an acquaintance from one of his clubs, a doctor who Anne's inquiries had indicated was widely regarded as second-rate. In addition, several people had mentioned his heavy drinking.

"He's got a smug, superior manner," said Anne. She added with an ironic smile, "Of course, that's my unsupported personal opinion, Inspector."

Dr. Fillington had spoken soothingly of "women's troubles" and had confided man-to-man to Eric that it was hardly surprising Charlotte wasn't coping . . . After all, an illegitimate child at sixteen . . . then unable to conceive when legally married. Add to this her insistence on a demanding career where she worked far too hard, her inability to successfully combine her wifely duties and her work . . . In his opinion a breakdown was only to be expected.

When asked to sum him up, Anne said,

"Patriarchal, patronizing and narrow-minded. And I don't believe he gave Mrs. Darcy even the most cursory examination. If he had, surely even he would have realized that drugs were a possibility. It seems to me Dr. Fillington simply took her husband's word for the situation and her behavior." She added indignantly, "And he prescribed tranquilizers, isn't that just amazing?"

Carol was thoughtful. "Perhaps Eric Higgins deliberately chose a doctor who wouldn't realize it was amphetamine abuse."

Anne's face was lit with fervor as she considered the implications. "But that would mean he knew his wife was on drugs — and he didn't want her off them." She shook her head. "But it doesn't make sense unless there was some advantage in it for him . . ."

"Work on it," said Carol, amused at the enthusiasm that had Anne almost instantly at her office door. "But before you do, I'd like the details on amphetamine intoxication Dr. Reed provided to you."

Anne ran rapidly through the points Dr. Reed had made. Carol was familiar with the symptoms, but it was useful to have them itemized by a doctor who specialized in patients with drug problems. The physical effects of high dosages of amphetamines included rapid heartbeat, high blood pressure, an elevated temperature and dilated pupils. Regarding the psychological effects, Dr. Reed had noted that true hallucinations were rare with amphetamine intoxication, although the main effects could be extreme. These were visual illusions, distortions of time and space, the experiencing of colors, textures, smells and tastes more sharply and vividly, and intense emotion that changed frequently and abruptly. Sometimes sensory perceptions might be blended, so the person heard colors and saw noises.

Dr. Reed's final point was that she had observed that patients often developed exaggerated empathy with others, or, conversely, became extremely detached in situations where a normal person might be expected to show a heightened emotional response.

Carol wondered if that had been included as an explanation of Charlotte Darcy's behavior when she was found by her brother's body.

Her thoughts were interrupted by the imperious ring of her telephone. "Aunt Sarah — I was going to call you."

She smiled at the exclamations that filled her ear. "Aunt, slow down. Yes, I'm on the case . . . No, I can't discuss it with you. Actually, I was wondering if we could visit you this weekend . . . Yes, Sybil too . . ."

* * * * *

"Let me tell you all about Bryce Darcy," said Bourke, regarding with suspicion the contents of his coffee mug.

They were sitting in Bourke's neat office, and Carol, who had opted for tea, grimaced as she swallowed a mouthful from her mug which was decorated with a hugely smiling Cheshire cat whose outlines were blurring around its sharply etched mouthful of teeth. A present from Sybil, it always reminded her of Sybil's portly ginger Jeffrey.

"I find it interesting," said Bourke, amused at Carol's distaste, "that we are quite prepared to drink tea or coffee at work that we wouldn't even look at anywhere else."

"True but irrelevant," said Carol, smiling with relief at the comfort of their old light banter. She had no wish to return to the unwelcome intensity of their last conversation and had been waiting warily to see if Bourke's manner would indicate any change in their relationship.

She said, "Now, what about Bryce Darcy?"

"Absolutely unremarkable in every way. Forty-two, an accountant, in good health, married to Wilma and the father of two boys, six and four. Played golf, belonged to the local chamber of commerce, was treasurer for the local historical society. Apparently completely law-abiding — not even a speeding ticket. He obviously didn't inherit his mother's artistic abilities but no doubt Keith saw him as a chip off the old block as far as the business was concerned because it seems he showed a real flair for marketing. From that point of view, his death is a considerable blow to the company."

"He didn't marry until his mid-thirties," said Carol, venturing another mouthful of her tea.

Bourke nodded. "That's not surprising. Everyone mentions him as being quiet and shy. He didn't seem to have any very close friends and certainly no enemies — he wasn't positive enough to create them."

"Eric Higgins didn't like his brother-in-law."

"Well, that's different, Carol. Hating relatives, particularly the ones you get by marriage, is perfectly normal behavior."

Ignoring his levity, Carol said, "Charlotte's husband had a better reason than that, didn't he?"

"Sure did," responded Bourke, handing her a stapled sheet. "There in all its glory is the financial state of Eric's Magic Video. Megan was quite right when she told us her stepfather's business is about to go down the gurgler. The only thing that's kept him afloat for so long has been injections of his wife's money, and Bryce was about to pull the plug on that."

"To give him a motive he would have had to know that Bryce was about to stop the cash."

"How about this scenario," said Bourke persuasively. "Bryce comes down to see his sister and tell her what's happening. You need to know that most of Charlotte's income from Darcy Designs goes into an investment trust — the others have a similar arrangement — and a substantial monthly allowance for immediate use is paid into her personal account. So, in comes Bryce to tell his sister he's going to stop this automatic payment each month to make it impossible for her to continue bankrolling Eric's failing business. She doesn't take kindly to her brother's interference. Unbalanced to begin with, this final straw lobs her right off her perch. Demented, she grabs the nearest weapon to hand and whacks him with it." He sat back, satisfied. "I like it," he said.

Carol moved her shoulders irritably. "You're absolutely convinced Charlotte Darcy killed her brother, aren't you?"

"Oh, come on, Carol. How many cases do we have where the obvious person *is* the murderer . . . and you know as well as I do that the Director of Public Prosecutions will probably let her cop a manslaughter charge . . . I can't see what your problem is."

"My problem," said Carol acidly, "is that I have serious doubts about her guilt." Before he could respond, she added, "And I have the uncomfortable feeling, Mark, that you're ignoring any evidence to the contrary."

He stared at her, astonished. "Carol, that just isn't true."

A heady rage, demanding the luxury of release, rose in her throat. She knew that it was unfair, that he had become the focus of her baffled anger, but even so, bitter thoughts about his attitude toward the case jostled to be expressed.

And if she stayed in his office she would say things she would later regret. She wanted to accuse him of a cop out — of not investigating closely because it was easier to find Charlotte Darcy guilty. She wanted to say: It's because she's a woman, Mark, and you're comfortable with the idea that women can be weak and irrational — that they can succumb to drugs and lose control and beat someone to death with a hammer . . .

"I'll speak to you later," she said, leaving him staring after her.

CHAPTER FIVE

The next morning was perfect winter weather, the windy chill of darkness replaced by the intoxicating warmth of a still, sunny morning that seemed to promise spring, short sleeves and open windows.

Buoyed by the radiance of the day, Carol pushed away her anger at Bourke's insistence on the likelihood of Charlotte Darcy's guilt. They drove the clogged highway to Parramatta enjoying a light-hearted conversation of shared memories. They had worked on many cases together and Carol felt a rush of affection as she looked at his blunt profile. He hadn't become that all too typical police officer — cynical, weary, inured to suffering and corruption. He had a fair-minded integrity, a logical, probing mind, a patient, even temperament.

She looked down at the street directory, wanting to say something to show how highly she regarded him, a throw-away line with a core of seriousness, but her usual fluency was absent. Instead she said, "It's the next on the left. Number forty-seven."

Wilma Darcy's sister, Darlene Fox, met them at the door with a suitably restrained manner. She led them into a lounge room filled with black vinyl furniture fatly puffed to look like leather and a confusion of glowing copper ornaments. Wilma Darcy was palely waiting, a magazine held in one listless hand.

Bryce's widow was small, slight, subtly appealing. Her large gray eyes dominated the delicate triangle of a face framed with soft flyaway light brown hair skillfully cut in casual wisps. Her mouth wasn't quite in balance with the rest of her, being thickly, moistly red. Carol noted that Wilma Darcy's black dress was undoubtedly expensive, that her shoes had the highest of heels, that ear lobes were almost non-existent and that her fingernails were so perfect they must be false.

"I've no idea who would have . . . who could have *wanted* to kill Bryce," she was saying in answer to Bourke's questioning. Her voice, an insinuating low-pitched timbre, was appropriate to the full fleshiness of her lips. "Sergeant, I feel frightened. What if it's someone with a grudge? Someone unbalanced? And the children — do you think they'll be safe?"

Carol was wryly amused at Bourke's soothing response, having the suspicion that Wilma Darcy was rather tougher than she looked. Carol had to admit she was not disposed to be generous to her, as she suspected Wilma was one of those women who always directed their full attention to any man present, wasting time on their own sex only when no masculine interest was available.

Involuntarily, Carol thought: Vicki Thorpe is the antithesis of this woman.

Forcing her attention back to the interview, Carol said, "Exactly when did you last see your husband?"

Wilma transferred her glance from Bourke. "Why, Monday morning, at breakfast. I believe a family should be together at the beginning of a day . . ." Her full mouth trembled as she looked back to Bourke. "The boys don't know what's happened, yet. They just think their Daddy's away."

Feeling guilty at her impatience with the bereaved wife, Carol said more gently, "Exactly what was discussed at breakfast, and when did he leave?"

"We talked about family things — where we'd go for our holidays. Then Bryce said he had to drive down to Sydney to see Charlotte. Said he'd spoken to her on the phone and she'd seemed much worse than before. He left about nine o'clock, I think, because my friend Jill had already picked up the boys for school before he said goodbye. We take it in turns, you see — to take the kids to the local school."

Bourke said, "Do you know if he intended to go straight to his sister's place?"

Wilma frowned at the question. "I suppose so. Why are you asking?"

"We know, even with heavy traffic, your husband wouldn't have taken more than a couple of hours to get to Baulkham Hills. The gardener spoke to him when he arrived at about one, so he obviously spent time somewhere else. Do you have any idea where that might be? Did he keep an appointment diary at home? He didn't have one with him."

Wilma spoke sharply. "I haven't seen a diary and I've no idea where he might have been. I suggest you check with his secretary."

Carol was intrigued by her hard-eyed response to what seemed an innocuous question. She indicated with a glance that Bourke was to continue. He said, his voice sympathetic, "It's difficult to ask you this under the circumstances but . . ." He paused diplomatically. "Were you and your husband entirely happy? Is there any possibility there was someone else?"

Wilma was vibrating with anger. "There was no one else! It's unthinkable. We had a very happy marriage. If you don't believe me, ask Bryce's family, ask my sister. They'll confirm what I say."

"We would like your permission to go through your husband's papers — anything he kept at home."

Her red mouth pursed in irritation, Wilma said, "I don't see why that's necessary." Encountering Bourke's pleasantly obstinate expression, she added, "Oh, all right, but I want to be there. I'm going back to the Blue Mountains early tomorrow with

Nora. The afternoon's the only time that'll suit me. I certainly don't want to be disturbed during the weekend."

*　*　*　*　*

Driving back to the city past Parramatta Road's garish used car blandishments, Carol and Bourke discussed the interview. "I'll bet she goes through her husband's papers with a fine tooth comb before she lets me near them," said Bourke.

"And his office at Darcy Designs?"

"Nothing that looks immediately interesting. We've taken his briefcase and the contents of his desk. He had a habit of scribbling cryptic notes to himself and I've got Anne checking out every last one of them. No result yet."

"And does Wilma Darcy figure on your list of suspects? Surely she meets the requirement of close family member," said Carol with a hint of asperity.

"Surely she's disqualified," Bourke said. "Clearly she's incapable of using a weapon that might put her fingernails, clothes or make-up at risk. But," he added more seriously, "I must say she isn't giving the impression of a woman broken by grief. Maybe *she's* the one with a lover, not her husband."

"Mark, you have such a high opinion of human nature," Carol said.

He responded with an ironic smile. "I put that down to the people we deal with every day. They're all such sterling citizens, aren't they — as they lie, cheat and occasionally murder each other . . ."

*　*　*　*　*

As Carol was packing her briefcase at the end of the day, Vicki Thorpe rang. "Yes, Vicki, I've got the printout with the information you wanted. Sybil's seeing you tomorrow, isn't she? I'll give it to her tonight, and she can pass it on."

Her mouth quirking in annoyance, she listened to Vicki's exuberant voice. "Look, Vicki, I've got no idea . . . I don't see how I can find out, and frankly, it doesn't seem particularly relevant. I'm sorry, I have to go . . ."

She broke the communication, standing with her hand resting on the receiver. Vicki's last question had been typically brash — "Carol, could you tell me how many gays and lesbians there are in the police force and what sort of discrimination they face? I'm doing a submission for the Equal Rights Commission on public servants . . ."

Carol snapped her briefcase shut, shaking her head. If I didn't know any better, she thought with black humor, I'd think Vicki Thorpe was working very hard to raise my lesbian consciousness.

* * * * *

The next morning Carol took Anne Newsome with her for the interview with Charlotte Darcy. She sat silent as Anne drove to Naomi Reed's clinic, her arms folded to contain the irritated restlessness that prickled under her skin. At this point in an investigation she was usually channeled, alert — her attention focused on making sense of the mass of apparently unrelated detail, comments, impressions. This time was different. She felt stale, unenthusiastic, negative — the bleakness highlighted by Constable Newsome's irksome eagerness to be fully involved in the investigation.

Carol frowned at Anne's profile, quite aware that she was being unjust. She could remember herself as a green constable, puppy-keen to solve some challenging crime, put on the "soft" areas of juvenile and domestic violence while male colleagues experienced the wider expanse of police work. She had had to work, and work hard, to get where she was now, fighting prejudice every step of the way.

Her resentment brought an ironic smile to her lips. Was she really so angry that a young woman like Anne Newsome had an easier time than she had had? Was there some intrinsic value in doing it the hard way?

"Something funny?" said Anne, who had caught her smile.

"Just contemplating my career," said Carol lightly.

The younger woman started to say something, stopped, then blurted, "Inspector, I want you to know — I've been meaning to say — you've been an example to me of what's possible. I mean, to use the jargon, you're a role model for women in the Force."

Taken aback, Carol was saved from the difficult task of replying by the discreet crunch of fine gravel as they drew up at the Reed Clinic's impressive entrance.

Waiting for Anne to park the car, Carol asked herself what possible reply she could have given to such an accolade. She was keenly aware that because so few women had yet attained high positions in the Force she must, by default, present an example. She thought savagely, *I don't want to be a role model for anyone.*

Naomi Reed herself greeted them briefly and handed them over to a white-coated assistant. The pastel halls were carpeted, glimpses of the extensive gardens could be seen from the wide windows that filled the building with light, huge bowls of flowers were displayed at appropriate intervals. There was little suggestion of a clinic for the treatment of mental illness or drug abuse — rather it seemed like a quietly sumptuous hotel. The assistant led them to a paneled door, knocked lightly, opened it and stood aside to allow them to enter.

Although she knew Charlotte Darcy's parents, Carol had never met Charlotte before. Stepping into the tastefully furnished room, Carol was immediately struck by the resemblance between daughter and mother. Megan was a younger version of the woman who stood passively regarding her.

Charlotte Darcy was tall, thin, almost gaunt, with dark eyes and black curly hair lightly streaked with gray. She wore a plain beige dress, flat heels and no jewelry. She had the same nervous, intense movements Carol had observed in her daughter, but there was humor in the set of her mouth and in the laughter-lines at the corners of her eyes.

Charlotte gestured for them to be seated in the pastel pink chairs arranged around a low marble table which held a vase full of luxuriantly blooming roses. Carol chose a chair that would allow her to keep her back to the light streaming in through the open window. Anne Newsome assumed a satellite position, close enough to take notes, but far enough away to indicate she was an attendant body.

After clearing her throat several times, Charlotte said without any introductory pleasantries, "Dr. Reed has told me that I've been under the influence of amphetamines. Before you ask me any questions I want to make it clear that I have no idea when and where I took these drugs or who gave them to me."

Carol's tone indicated mild interest. "And have you been taking any medication recently?"

"No. I take aspirin occasionally if I have a headache, but otherwise I avoid medicines of any kind."

Mentally checking through the neatly typed inventory of items in the Darcys' bathroom cabinet, Carol said, "Vitamin supplements? Anything like that?"

Charlotte shrugged wearily. "I take a multi-vitamin capsule when I remember to . . . I often skip meals, and Eric is always complaining I don't have a proper diet."

Carol became businesslike. "Amphetamines can be injected, or taken in powder, capsule or tablet form. Since it's possible you've been under the influence of these drugs for some time, and you say you haven't knowingly taken anything, how would you explain what's happened?"

Charlotte bowed her head. "It's a mistake. It must be. Otherwise I have to believe that someone would do it deliberately — give me something to make me think I was going mad."

Wanting to put her at ease, Carol leaned back into the comfort of the plushly upholstered chair, saying sympathetically, "It must have been very disturbing to have these mood swings and not know why."

"Disturbing?" said Charlotte with derision. "That hardly seems strong enough. At the end I was terrified. My feelings were so intense, so uncontrollable. And I sometimes saw things that I knew weren't there." Slowly shaking her head, she added, "It was so confusing — time seemed distorted and I began to feel I couldn't rely on anything to be real." She looked at Anne Newsome, who was diligently making notes. "You're getting this all down, are you? That I wasn't responsible for what I did?"

"What did you do?"

Charlotte seemed transfixed by Carol's quiet question, staring at her for several moments. Then she said, "Eric tells me I was found with Bryce's body. He thinks I told a police officer I had killed my brother. Is that true? Did I say that?"

"Do you remember that afternoon?" She was careful to sound reasonable and restrained, to make no gestures, to present no threat.

Charlotte pressed her knuckles to her mouth. "Why would I say that, Inspector?"

Carol was matter-of-fact. "You were sitting on a work stool next to your brother's body. The weapon used — a hammer — was beside you. You had blood on your clothes. One of the patrol officers first on the scene asked if you had attacked your brother. You replied, 'I must have — I don't remember.' "

Charlotte stared at her, unspeaking. The ripple of a page turning in Anne Newsome's notebook sounded loud in the silence.

"What *do* you remember?" said Carol when it was obvious that Charlotte was not going to respond.

Taking a deep breath, Charlotte said, "I remember some things, but they're like disconnected scenes from a movie. I think I remember finding Bryce's body lying there with the blood on his head . . ." Her eyes filling with tears, she groped for a handkerchief. "I'm sorry, I can't get used to the fact that he's gone, that I'll never see him again."

Carol's voice was gentle, her posture relaxed. "If you can, will you tell us any snatches of memory you have."

"Bryce called me from the Blue Mountains and said he wanted to see me urgently. I remember answering the phone and I remember that he sounded upset. It was a personal problem and he said something like, 'You will listen to me today, Lottie, won't you?'"

"That sounds like he'd raised the subject before."

"If he did, I don't remember."

Suddenly impatient, Carol leaned forward. "So you have no idea what your brother wanted to discuss with you?"

Spreading her large hands, Charlotte said with a vestige of humor, "For once, it wasn't my behavior, I'm sure of that. Bryce had something he wanted to tell me."

Carol relaxed again, forcing a note of sympathy into her voice. "You and your brother were close?"

"Close?" Charlotte's glance wandered to the vase bursting with warm colored blooms. Her mouth twisted in a bitter smile. "They choose the colors to soothe the mind. That's why the walls in here are pale pink, the carpet a shade of rose. Did you know those colors are supposed to lift depression?"

"Yes," said Carol, and waited.

"Manic patients have cool colors — blues, greens." Charlotte glanced at Anne Newsome. "Are you taking this down, Constable? It could be helpful information." She smiled slightly at Anne's patient expression, then said to Carol, "Bryce and I were very close when I was young. I suppose you've met Megan. I was sixteen when I found I was pregnant and Bryce was wonderful to me. There was only a year between us, but he was my older brother and I looked up to him. He gave me advice and support . . ."

"And lately?"

Charlotte grimaced. "Bryce was never happy about my marriage to Eric. It meant that I saw less of my brother, socially at least. There was always a barrier between us."

"Your husband's attitude?"

"It was a mutual dislike."

Carol was stabbed with a sour distaste for the relentless probing she must do. "We've questioned your brother's wife."

Sardonic amusement flickered over Charlotte's face. "The ever-feminine Wilma?" To Carol's acknowledging smile she said, "She's a piranha. You notice her sharp little teeth?"

Anne looked up as Carol said laughingly, "She didn't pay me very much attention. Detective Sergeant Bourke was with me during the interview."

Charlotte's expression showed this was explanation enough. "She used to treat Dad that way too, but something's gone wrong just recently. Lately he's become immune to her wide-eyed aren't-you-wonderful look, although I don't know why. Wilma usually plays her cards well."

"You're not fond of your sister-in-law?" said Carol, hoping to disarm with the mild amusement in her voice.

"I'm indifferent — and so is Wilma. We looked upon each other as a necessary evil, I suppose." Charlotte smiled wearily. "And that's all I'm willing to say about anything, Inspector. I'm incriminated enough, aren't I?"

Carol felt a rush of pity for the woman who faced her with ironic humor at a time when she must be, at the very least, apprehensive about her future.

Carol stood, bringing Anne Newsome to her feet also. "We'll leave you now," she said gently. "There'll be some other questions later, when you're feeling better."

"Better?"

The word still held its derisive sting when Carol left the room. Even if Charlotte Darcy had killed her brother, the cost must be greater than she could have imagined. And, more and more, Carol's belief in her innocence was hardening. She dismissed the thought that it was a conviction based on sympathy, saying to Anne, "What do you think? Guilty or not?"

Anne smiled at her. "Unfair question, Inspector. I like her, so I don't want her to be guilty. That doesn't mean she isn't."

"And her story that she's been fed amphetamines without her knowledge?"

"In powder form amphetamines have a salty, acrid flavor. If what she says is true, either she was given her doses in capsules or tablets or the taste was disguised in some way."

Carol was interested in Anne's opinion. "Do you believe she was drugged without her knowledge, or do you think she's feeding us a line?"

Anne sighed. "I'd like to believe her, I really would, but it's just too far-fetched. The simple answer's usually the right one, isn't it? She's hooked on speed and things got out of control. Maybe she doesn't remember killing her brother — but I think she did it."

Angry with herself for feeling a sense of betrayal that Anne's opinion so closely mirrored Mark Bourke's, Carol said shortly, "We need to know a lot more about Bryce Darcy before we can be sure there isn't someone out there with a compelling motive to kill him. His sister's drug addiction might be incidental."

"Where did she get the speed?" said Anne. "Who was supplying her? Of course, drugs are easy to get if you know where to ask . . ." She paused in thought, then said, "What about her daughter, Megan? *She'd* move in the sort of circles where drugs are widely available, don't you think?"

"I presume Mark's checking that out," said Carol, her tone indicating she wanted no further discussion.

She had noticed Anne took cues well. Anne looked thoughtfully at Carol, and said nothing further.

*   *   *   *   *

Are you trying to placate me? thought Carol as she noticed that Mark Bourke had placed Charlotte second last on the time chart he had left on her desk.

Bryce Darcy had died between two and three o'clock on Monday afternoon, the gardener confirming his arrival at his sister's house at Baulkham Hills at approximately one o'clock.

Bryce's parents, Keith and Nora, had driven down from Katoomba late on Sunday afternoon to stay in their Sydney apartment for the first half of the week. On Monday Keith had several business appointments and Nora took the opportunity to meet a friend and to shop. The two of them had returned to their Hyde Park apartment when Eric Higgins had called after three-thirty with the news of their son's death. Bourke had noted: *Checking on Keith's appointments. Nora Darcy met a friend for coffee in the morning, but was alone after that.*

Wilma Darcy was in Katoomba, a hundred kilometers from Sydney and at least eighty kilometers from Baulkham Hills where her husband was murdered. She had an arrangement with a neighbor to share the task of driving their children to and from school and on Monday afternoon it had been her turn to pick up her boys and the neighbor's son and daughter at three o'clock.

Megan Darcy had been attending lectures and tutorials at Sydney University from one o'clock until four. Her tutor in American literature, Malcolm Plassy, had vouched for her attendance at his tutorial from one to two.

Charlotte Darcy had been alone at home. The gardener had noticed her walking near the ornamental pond about midday, but when Bryce arrived an hour later she had apparently gone inside. The next person to report seeing her was Eric Higgins when he discovered her with her brother's body.

Eric Higgins had been visiting his three video outlets. Bourke had noted: *It might be possible for him to return home between the meetings with his staff at the three outlets. Time would be tight, but he could do it.*

In a final note, Bourke reported that a doorknock of neighboring properties had been fruitless as the few people home at the time had seen or heard nothing unusual. Similarly the local police station had experienced a standard Monday with traffic problems and minor misdemeanors the only things of note.

Carol was reading the final detailed autopsy report on Bryce Darcy when Bourke appeared in the doorway wearing a well-cut dark blue suit and a red tie. "Leaving to keep my appointment with Widow Darcy in Katoomba," he said cheerfully.

"I like the suit, Mark," said Carol, curious about what was, for Bourke, a considerable departure from his usual shades of brown and beige.

He looked pleased but discomforted. "Pat thought I needed a change."

However close professionally, Carol and Bourke had always respected each other's privacy. But now, tentatively, Bourke seemed to be making attempts to change the unspoken rules. Carol wanted to keep the relationship as it had always been, yet she was warmed by his disclosure. She said lightly, without real sincerity, "I'd like to meet Pat."

He said carefully, "That'd be great. Perhaps you and Sybil . . ."

Carol recoiled from the implication in his words, but her expression didn't change. "Maybe after this case is wrapped up," she said, deliberately vague.

He started to say something, then apparently thought better of it. "Call you if I find anything interesting in Bryce's papers," he said as he turned away.

Carol sat staring at the empty doorway. Mark Bourke had known about Carol's relationship with Sybil for a long time — she could accept that. But to socialize with him, to openly court the possibility that more and more people with whom she worked would become familiar with the secrets of her private life . . .

She took a deep breath and shoved the problem aside. Why disturb the status quo? Just leave things as they are.

Yet, as she turned back to the report, she was uneasily aware that her ability to exert control was limited. As Sybil turned outward, growing in confidence and experience, becoming more secure in her perceptions of herself, Carol realized that her own efforts were devoted to maintaining the walls she had built to protect her life.

CHAPTER SIX

In the bleak, cold light of Saturday morning, Carol couldn't force herself out of bed to take her usual early morning jog, telling herself that she would run in the evening along one of the Blue Mountains scenic trails near her Aunt Sarah's house at Leura.

"This has got to be better than jogging out there in the freezing cold," said Sybil as she snuggled against Carol's bare skin.

Carol slid back into the delicious state of sensuous half-waking, half-sleeping, the length of

Sybil's body against her own, the warmth of Sybil's breath tickling the hollow of her throat. A familiar heat began to flood her — tingling, demanding, quickening her heart.

"Oh, God," said Sybil, laughing as she stretched in Carol's tightening embrace. "Don't tell me you lust after me *again*."

Carol turned to lie on top of her, mouth hungry for sensation. "You should be so lucky," she said. "You just happen to be handy, that's all."

The welcome oblivion of passion enveloped her as she felt Sybil's lips opening to the demands of her thrusting tongue, Sybil's thigh pushed hard between her legs.

Sybil responded to her lead, followed her desire, rose up to meet her orgasm. And yet, as Carol's breathing slowed so did her elation in the ephemeral release she had gained.

Sybil was compliant, accommodating, never rejecting. But their relationship had somehow dulled from the sharp delight it had once contained. She was abruptly aware that she no longer asked what Sybil was thinking or feeling.

She thought: Am I so absorbed in myself that I've let Sybil become an adjunct to my life? "Darling?" she said, but Sybil was asleep.

* * * * *

The Great Western Highway was heavy with Saturday morning drivers intent on their weekend pursuits, rather than the usual commuting to work. This seemed to make them less impatient but more erratic. Sybil swore when one particular driver changed lanes for the third time without any indication of his intention.

"Where are the police when you need them?" she demanded, glaring at the offending car.

Carol, sitting relaxed beside her in an olive green tracksuit, smiled. "You've got your very own Detective Inspector, darling. What more do you want?"

Suddenly serious, Sybil said, "I want you to want more."

"Meaning?"

"Carol, you've shut yourself away. How many people are you close to . . . *really* close to?"

Keeping her voice light, Carol said, "What is this? Quantity versus quality?"

Obviously determined not to let Carol evade the issue, Sybil said, "You have your work, you have me, and you see your son, once every week or so. And there's a few rather remote friends and acquaintances. That's it, isn't it?"

"It's all I want."

Sybil drove in silence for a few moments. Then she said, "You're not fair to me."

Carol didn't want to consider the weight of that remark. She thought, I'm willing to discuss this, but not now. Then, more honestly — I'm willing to discuss it, but only on my terms.

Baffled by how she should respond, she said sharply, "How am I not fair? I don't tell *you* how to run your life or who to see or not to see, do I?"

"I feel you've got all your emotional eggs in one basket — and it's me."

Unwilling to consider the implications of the statement, Carol said coldly, "So your problem is that I love you. Is that it?"

Sybil didn't respond, sounding the horn as yet another motorist earned her censure.

Carol sat silent, angry with herself, angry that Sybil had brought up the subject, angry that her pleasure in Sybil's company had been soured. Finally she said, "Are you going to answer me?"

Sybil said gently, "I don't know how to answer you, Carol."

"I gather you want me to make changes in my life, even though I'm quite content the way it is."

Sybil sighed, ran a hand through her curly red hair, looked sideways at Carol's frown. "Are you really content?"

Carol broke another uncomfortable pause by saying, "The other day Mark asked me if I was thinking of resigning from the Force."

Sybil glanced at her quickly. "Why did he ask that? Are you?"

Carol shrugged, saying offhandedly, "He said something about getting the impression I was unhappy, discontented . . ."

"Carol, you know I'll support you in anything you decide to do."

"Even resigning?"

"Have you seriously considered it?"

Carol stared unseeingly out the window, twisting her black opal ring with inattentive compulsion. She said flatly, "The thought had crossed my mind. I can't say I really considered it until Mark said something. Now . . . I don't know. I'd rather not talk about it at the moment. Okay?"

Sybil reached over and squeezed her hand. "Okay."

* * * * *

As the Great Western Highway commenced its ascent into the Blue Mountains, Carol's spirits began a corresponding rise. The mountain town of Leura, where her Aunt Sarah lived, symbolized the essence of the long, hot summers of her childhood — summers remembered as a succession of perfect, sun-drenched days stretching over the bliss of the long Christmas break from school.

Carol's love for Aunt Sarah, her mother's only sister, was uncomplicated by duty or expectations. Even as an adult, she had turned to Aunt Sarah when her parents had died — first her father from a heart attack, then her mother in a grieving surrender to the cancer she had been battling successfully until her husband's death.

Carol smiled as she caught the first glimpses of the warm ocher of the sandstone cliffs that rose out of the wide valley floors of the Blue Mountains National Park. She turned to Sybil with sudden delighted zest. "Darling, let's go to Echo Point early tomorrow morning, then all the way down the Giant's Staircase and around the base of the cliffs to the Scenic Railway."

Sybil, reacting to Carol's elation, laughed. "Sounds energetic."

Carol responded with mock severity. "The last time I was about twelve . . . and I did it the hard way. We went down the Scenic Railway and climbed the thousand or so steps of the Giant's Staircase. Be thankful I'm not suggesting we do it in that order."

Sybil turned the car off the highway, over the railway line and into Leura's charming main street, which had been restored to the grace of its early century self, and held refurbished gift, craft and antique shops, small art galleries and an abundance of tearooms beckoning to the passing person. Even before Leura's renaissance, Carol remembered her childhood delight in walking up one side of the street and down the other, peering into the shops, speculating about the visitors who came in dust-covered cars from unsealed roads, counting precious coins for an ice cream or sweets.

Aunt Sarah lived near the Gordon Falls, a spectacular drop of feathered water disappearing into the dark green-gray of the bushland lapping the foot of the sheer sandstone cliffs. Her house was typical of the old style Blue Mountains' dwelling — painted weatherboard with a wide veranda on two sides. The corrugated iron roofing fitted the building like a tight hat, curling into a smooth curve where it met the gutter running along the veranda, its wooden supports boasting elaborate carved pieces.

Carol remembered long summer evenings sitting with her aunt and uncle on ancient wooden chairs set on the creaking boards of the veranda. As they waited for the promised southerly change to blow the oven hot air of the day away, her uncle would smoke a pipe, her aunt would often shell peas. Then later, going inside, blinking in the harshness of artificial light after the mellow softness of the darkness, sinking into the high old bed whose mattress had a distinct dip in the middle, dreaming of the splendid uncertainties of the future.

Sybil stopped the car and Aunt Sarah came leaping down the four stone steps in welcome. The mountain air was still, cold, uncontaminated by noise or pollution. "Aunt!" said Carol, gladly submitting to the familiar firm hug.

After squeezing Sybil in a similar embrace, Aunt Sarah bustled them inside. "Tea, scones and a talk — and in that order," she announced.

The kitchen was a warm, welcoming room, dominated by a gargantuan antique wooden table with a surface scrubbed by generations until it was full of dips and grooves. The kitchen chairs were of similar vintage, uncompromisingly utilitarian and constructed to take the weight of the heaviest individual.

Carol looked affectionately at the familiar figure bustling to complete the rituals of afternoon tea. Aunt Sarah was short, comfortably plump and possessed of buoyant energy. She spoke rapidly, often failing to finish one sentence before she began the next. Her gestures were flamboyant and her clothes unconventional — Carol smiled at the capacious magenta overalls and a mauve blouse covered with large purple blossoms. Her skin, so deeply tanned it retained its color even in winter, fanned in a network of wrinkles around her eyes, which were green, like Carol's, but of a lighter, washed out shade, as though a lifetime of harsh sunlight had faded them.

"There!" Aunt Sarah exclaimed, slapping thick

white mugs on the table, then turning to take scones from the oven. "Have it while it's hot."

Sybil said innocently, "Carol might like coffee."

"Nonsense! Heard more about the pernicious effects of caffeine the other day. Heart racing, cholesterol up, stomach disturbed. Won't have it in the house, as you know very well."

"Don't bait my aunt," said Carol with mock disapproval.

She could feel herself relaxing as her childhood memories of this room melded with the present. She could remember so many summer holidays in the Blue Mountains, playing with the neighborhood kids, walking the countless bush trails, splashing in the Leura Cascades, the tingling excitement of exploring the imaginary — and real — dangers of the rift valleys below the settlements on the heights. Returning in the late afternoon to always find in this kitchen home-made biscuits, cordial, and an interested audience for her recitals of the day's adventures.

Of course some things had changed: Aunt Sarah's hair was now white, although still styled in a careless halo around her head; Uncle Paul's pencil-thin presence was gone, folded into an unexpectedly early grave; Georgette, her aunt's beloved Siamese cat, had gone to feline heaven; the brooding black iron stove had been replaced with a sleek and superior electric model. Otherwise everything was the same — the worn linoleum with its elaborate but faded pattern, the row of cups and mugs hanging on hooks under the thick wooden shelf above the sink, the fleshy preserved fruits smugly displaying themselves in glass jars. Carol remembered several occasions when she had set out to help Aunt Sarah with her fruit bottling, only to be banished from the steamy kitchen when her aunt became too exasperated by Carol's fumbling efforts.

"Nora Darcy's been to see me," announced Aunt Sarah. "And she's begged, pleaded even, for me to intercede."

"Oh, yes?" said Carol.

Her aunt grinned at her noncommittal tone. "I said to her — Nora, it's hopeless asking me to try and influence Carol. She has her duty to do, but I'm sure she'll at least listen." Switching her attention to Sybil, she added, "Do *you* have any success? I know I can never get Carol to do what I want."

Carol said with patient amusement, "I can't really discuss that Darcy case with you, Aunt."

"Of course you can't, but *I* can mention it to you. Nora and Keith are distraught, of course. They both think your Detective Sergeant Bourke is going to arrest Charlotte for Bryce's murder . . ."

As Aunt Sarah paused to assess the impact of her words, Carol sipped her tea, her face expressionless.

"Then who killed him?" asked Sybil as she spread butter thickly on a steaming scone.

"Well, an intruder, of course. Some burglar, a drug addict looking for money . . ."

Carol regarded her speculatively. "And what do *you* think, Aunt Sarah?" When her aunt looked discomfited, she added, "Come on, be truthful."

"Well, Nora's told me about the amphetamines — can't say I was surprised — I know Charlotte's been a bit strange lately . . ." Aunt Sarah, usually so positive, was being evasive.

"And?"

Throwing up her hands, Aunt Sarah said with irritation, "All right! I won't quibble. If you must know, I think Charlotte's crazy. I don't mean it's permanent — but she's not normal . . ."

Carol continued to look expectantly at her.

Her aunt's breath gusted in a sigh. "And I think it's possible she went completely off the rails and attacked Bryce. If she could do that . . . well, she couldn't be mentally competent, could she? I mean, she wouldn't know what she'd done." She put her hand on Carol's shoulder. "And then it wouldn't be murder, would it?"

Carol put her fingers over her aunt's for a moment. "Do her parents privately share your view about their daughter?"

Aunt Sarah shook her head emphatically. "No way. They believe absolutely that someone else killed him."

"Why would anyone murder Bryce Darcy?"

"Well, that's *it,* Carol! No one normal would . . . no one that knew him, anyway."

"Most victims know their murderers — it's often a family member. And they don't kill because they're insane. It's often a spur of the moment thing, a total loss of control."

Aunt Sarah dismissed this remark with an impatient gesture. "Every family has differences — doesn't mean much. Your mother and I fought like cats and dogs. Loved each other, though." She glared at her niece. "If Charlotte *did* kill her brother, you can be sure she was quite mad at the time she did it."

Carol accepted another scone from Sybil.

Watching the butter melt onto the hot interior whiteness, she said casually, "Charlotte's a patient in Dr. Naomi Reed's clinic. Keith Darcy arrived with the doctor at the murder scene. This rather suggests a strong connection with the Darcy family . . ."

"You're as transparent as glass — you always have been," Aunt Sarah hooted. "Why don't you come straight out and ask the question, eh?"

Carol grinned. "Well? You know everything, my dear Aunt."

The reply was complacent. "It just so happens I do, at least in this case. Fact is, Naomi Reed's been treating Nora on and off for years."

"Nora?"

"Surprised, eh? I wouldn't tell you, except you'll ferret it out anyway. Nora's got a drinking problem. It's one of the reasons her creative work fell off and Charlotte had to take over everything."

Facts shifted and realigned. Carol said, "Nora Darcy's a recovered alcoholic. Is that right?"

"She's dry, if that's what you mean. God knows for how long with the strain she's under now. It's the uncertainty that eats away at you. That's why it's better, Carol, if you settle it once and for all. If Charlotte did it, arrest her and get it over with." Responding to Carol's stony glance, she added, "And I'm not trying to tell you what to do — pity help anyone who does that — it's just that the whole Darcy family is going to fall apart if this thing isn't resolved soon."

Carol said, "Tell me about Bryce's wife."

"Wilma? Not much to say. As marriages go, it seemed okay, and both of them adored the boys."

Carol idly played with the spoon in the

homemade jam until Aunt Sarah, in a gesture long remembered, lightly slapped her fingers and took temptation away from her. She sat back and folded her arms. "How did Wilma get on with the Darcy family?"

"In-laws," said Aunt Sarah darkly, "are often the cause of a serious rift. I know, I've been through it, but that's another story."

"Wilma has no problems with her father-in-law?"

A shrug accompanied the reply. "A bit of friction lately because Wilma wants to move to Sydney, but other than that everything's fine. If you want a *real* problem you don't have to look further than Eric Higgins."

"Meaning?"

"Keith hardly wastes a thought on Charlotte's husband. If anything, he's bored by him. But Bryce . . . Bryce couldn't stand Eric Higgins. Never seen him take such a dislike to anyone before, and I've known him since he was a kid. Don't mean he was rude, or they argued in front of anyone — Bryce wouldn't embarrass his sister. What he did do was avoid Eric like the plague. When they had to speak, Bryce was polite, cold — not a bit like his normal self."

Carol was interested to know if her aunt had heard any rumors about Eric Higgins that might explain Bryce's dislike of his brother-in-law. Although disappointed to admit she drew a blank on this subject, Aunt Sarah announced that she did have something she thought Carol should know. "I don't know if anyone else's noticed it, but there'd been quite a change in Bryce lately."

"Perhaps worry about his sister?"

Aunt Sarah pursed her lips in thought. "I didn't get the impression he was *worried*, exactly. More excited or disturbed. As if something unusual, something that was going to make a difference to his life, was happening."

"Obviously an affair," volunteered Sybil, who had been listening with interest.

"Maybe, but you'd think Wilma'd keep him occupied." Turning to Carol she went on, "She's got that look about her, don't you think? Insatiable, I mean."

Carol narrowed her eyes, visualizing Wilma as she had been in the interview. Insatiable wasn't quite the right word . . . more that she was hungry. Hungry for something — or someone.

On impulse, she said to her aunt, "Have you met Wilma Darcy's sister? She lives in Parramatta."

"Darlene Fox, the pale washed-out one? Wilma's had her up here at Christmas a couple of times. A single mother, you know — husband walked out on her when the second baby was born."

Carol said casually, "Are they close, as sisters go?"

Grinning wolfishly, Aunt Sarah said, "In a roundabout way I suppose you're asking me if Darlene would lie for Wilma — the answer's yes, like a shot. Wilma's the success story of the family and must be supported. She married up in the world, you see."

"Married up?" said Carol to encourage her aunt. Aunt Sarah, she wasn't at all surprised to find, had all the details.

"You wouldn't think it, to see Wilma now, but she came from a very poor background — no money and not much education. Her father was a laborer. Working for Katoomba Council when he died. Wilma and Darlene were just kids. Their mother worked as a waitress to support the family. The girls had to find jobs as soon as they were old enough." She stopped to look severely at Carol. "See how easy you had it?" she said.

"Wilma . . . ?" prompted Carol.

"Well, Wilma was always the sharp one. Served in a shop during the day, in the evening put herself through secretarial and bookkeeping courses. And she studied how to dress and how to behave like it was a university degree. It all paid off when she snapped up poor Bryce."

Carol thought of the determination and sheer hard work that Wilma had put into transforming her life. After that single-minded commitment, what might Wilma be prepared to do to keep what she had gained?

* * * * *

As the sun set, Carol, Sybil and Aunt Sarah put on jackets to brave the metallic chill of the backyard. They stood watching the flurry of colored wings and discordant voices as the native birds fed on the bird table. Carol could remember, as a child, her Uncle Paul casually throwing scraps onto the grass, but now Aunt Sarah was staunchly active in a wildlife preservation group, distributing stern leaflets written in her own inimitable style on the subject of the appropriate food to provide for native birds.

"Strictly speaking, I shouldn't do this, you know," her aunt said as she gestured at the large wooden bird table standing on a single slippery metal pole. "Should leave them to their own devices — but I can't resist because they're so beautiful. Mind, it's a special mixture — the proper balance of protein, carbohydrates and vitamins. I know you feed birds at your place, Carol. Have you got my leaflet?"

"Multiple copies."

Aunt Sarah grinned at her niece's resigned tone. "Then give them to friends. We've got to educate the public."

The slope of the backyard made it easy to see the top of the bird table. At one end was a shallow sunken bath, at the other a cacophony of colored birds squabbled over food. Carol's favorites were the Gang-gang Cockatoos, her pleasure in them based not on their flashy feathers — they were comparatively subdued, having slate gray bodies and a scarlet head garnished with a rather untidy red crest — but on their unmistakable creaky voices which reminded her of unoiled hinges.

As she smiled at the competition between the Gan-gangs and the rich red and blue Crimson Rosellas whose brassy cries concealed craven hearts — easily alarmed, they would flee for cover at even a hint of danger — they rose with a beat of frantic wings as someone came around the side of the house.

Megan Darcy stood, unspeaking, and looking truculent, as Aunt Sarah moved to kiss her cheek. She returned the embrace perfunctorily, saying to Carol, "Inspector, my grandfather wants to see you. When will you be free?"

Aunt Sarah's voice was tart. "Keith could have used the telephone."

"I said I'd bring the message, Aunt Sarah, because I wanted to say hello."

Carol felt a trace of vexation as she noted the familiarity with which Megan used Aunt Sarah's name, a feeling which intensified as she saw Megan regarding Sybil questioningly.

Aunt Sarah responded with the appropriate introductions and then led the way inside. "It's freezing out here. Come in and have a drink."

Carol was used to her aunt's policy of pouring lethal quantities of alcohol, so to ensure some sobriety she took over bar duties. Aunt Sarah shepherded Sybil and Megan towards the crackling heat of an open fire in what was always called the family room. It was filled with comfortable, shabby furniture, a startlingly modern television set and sound system, and the mementos of a crowded life, the heavy wooden mantelpiece above the satisfyingly robust fire crowded with faded photographs. In one photo an arrestingly beautiful young Sarah stared confidently into the room. Seeing Sybil's attention caught by this, Aunt Sarah said with satisfaction, "Not bad, eh? You can see Carol gets her looks from my side of the family."

As she went on to point out other salient photographs, Carol took the opportunity to assess Charlotte's daughter. Megan sat staring thoughtfully into the fire, ignoring the rum and Coke cradled in her hands. She wore faded jeans, stained sneakers and a fluorescent red pullover that accented the darkness of her hair. She turned, caught Carol's glance, and said, "She won't let me smoke in here — she's good for me, your aunt."

Wanting to form a bridge of common experience,

Carol said, "She's good for me, too. I always turn to her when I'm in trouble."

"You? In trouble?"

Carol's lips twitched. "Even Detective Inspectors have problems."

Megan frowned, straightened, took a large gulp from her glass. "Your problem at the moment, I imagine, is that you haven't got enough to arrest my mother."

"The investigation is to solve your Uncle Bryce's murder, not hang it on the nearest convenient suspect."

Carol's reasonable tone seemed to inflame Megan. She stood up abruptly, her face flushing with anger. "Then why aren't you concentrating on Eric Higgins? He's the bastard that did it!" She glared at Carol. "And my poor, bloody mother, half out of her mind with drugs, gets blamed. Fuck your investigation!"

"Language, Megan," said Aunt Sarah severely.

Megan took a deep breath and said in a more moderate tone, "I must go. Will you see my grandfather? Please — it's important to him. I'll pick you up after dinner tonight. Yes?"

Carol was willing to agree to the request. She wanted to observe Keith and Nora Darcy in their normal home environment, because that was usually where people were less guarded in their responses.

Dispatching Megan into the chill night, Aunt Sarah returned to say, "Do you know Megan thought Keith and Nora were her parents until she was about eleven or twelve? She believed Charlotte and Bryce were her much older sister and brother."

She smiled at Carol's interrogative expression. "See, your old aunt can be of use after all. Fact is,

Charlotte had the baby when she was sixteen and Keith insisted he and Nora bring Megan up as their own. Keith doted on her. Still does. She'll be his heir, you know. I'd bet big money on it."

"Who was the real father?"

"That I don't know. The pregnancy was hushed up and Charlotte sent away to have the child in secret. Often wondered if it was rape, or something like that."

"Incest?" said Carol.

Her aunt looked genuinely shocked. "This police work gives you a dirty mind," she said disapprovingly. "I suppose you're thinking Keith or Bryce fathered Megan, are you?"

"It has happened."

"Not this time, Carol. And I'd put my money on *that.*"

Carol, intrigued, said, "How did Megan take the news that the person she thought was her sister was actually her mother?"

"Not very well. Kicked up a hell of a fuss, in fact. Ran away from home, got as far as Kings Cross in Sydney before she was found."

"And now?"

Aunt Sarah grinned. "You've met her, my dear. Strike you as the life and soul of the party? She's full of resentment — and some of it's justified. Gives everyone in the family a hard time. Keith she blames for lying to her. Nora she thinks is weak because she went along with the pretense. Charlotte, her real mother, she loves with a kind of reluctant affection. Frankly, of all of them, I think she blamed Bryce the most. Has this idea he used emotional blackmail to persuade the family to hide Charlotte's pregnancy by sending her overseas. You can tell her she's wrong — and I have — but she won't listen, of course."

Seeing Carol's thoughtful expression, she added, "And don't go making her a suspect for Bryce's murder. Resentment is one thing — killing's another. Besides, I'm convinced Megan's got a lot more pleasure out of being a rebel and having confrontations with the family. Why spoil everything by knocking off your chief target?"

* * * * *

Katoomba, where the Darcys lived, adjoined Leura, both towns sitting on the lip of the sandstone cliffs, facing south over the huge wild expanses of the Jamison and Kedumba Valleys. Megan collected Carol at nine o'clock and then drove the red Mercedes sports car with insolent impetuosity, accelerating too fast, braking too hard, cornering with squealing tires. If she hoped to goad her passenger into complaint she was disappointed. Carol, hiding a smile, faced the short trip with equanimity and gravely thanked her when they jolted to a halt in front of a house that looked both alien and pretentious.

Carol remembered having seen photographs of the Darcy home in magazines. The architect who designed it clearly had had more desire to excite comment than to create a dwelling at home in the mountain landscape. The building basked in floodlighting, showing its extravagance of flat gray walls set at disconcerting angles, its tinted glass and swooping cantilevered roofs. Well above ground level a series of exaggerated bay windows jutted out pugnaciously.

Megan had been watching Carol's face as she surveyed the house. "Absolute monstrosity, isn't it?"

Carol could only agree. "Unusual," she said diplomatically.

"All Grandfather's idea, of course," said Megan as she led the way up a series of shallow steps to a front door largely composed of irregular pieces of brightly colored glass. "Gran nearly had a fit, but it was all fait accompli before she knew what was happening." She waved her hand vaguely off into the darkness. "Over there's the old house . . . it wasn't sold. I live in it now, when I'm not in Sydney."

Keith Darcy met Carol gravely, took her hand for a moment. "Carol, I appreciate you taking the time to see me." He nodded a dismissal to Megan, who quickly walked away towards the back of the house.

He was wearing what Carol categorized as formal casual wear — tailored slacks, leather slip-on shoes, a tweed jacket with leather patches at the elbows and a carefully arranged paisley cravat. With his weather-beaten skin, short graying hair and mustache, he looked like a gentleman farmer, lacking only a shotgun in the crook of his arm to complete the picture.

Carol, herself wanting to create a relaxed impression, had been careful to dress informally in tailored dark blue pants, short boots and a cerulean sweater.

He led the way through the air-conditioned vastness of the house, their feet clattering on the polished wooden floors. He was obviously proud of his home, stopping several times to point out some architectural feature for her appreciation. Finally they reached his study, a room intended to replicate the atmosphere of an exclusive British men's club. Everything was in dull dark tones, from the maroon leather furniture to the dark paneled walls. The chairs looked fat, shiny and uncomfortable and the dark green-shaded lamps cast pallid circles of light on their thickly padded arms.

"I'd like this to be just an informal chat," he said as he ushered her into the cool embrace of one of the overweight chairs. It didn't give beneath her weight and she had a ridiculous fancy that if she leaned back too confidently the chair would close around her and hold her captive.

He busied himself with a bottle of Haig's Dimple Scotch and an imposing silver soda siphon. His hands were clumsy, and the heavy cut-glass tumbler nearly slipped from his fingers as he handed it to her. "Sarah tells me you have a taste for whiskey," he said with unconvincing heartiness.

Carol smiled politely, content to wait. She sipped her whiskey and watched him prepare his own drink. He apologized as an ice cube escaped the silver tongs to skitter under a heavy dark desk which was undoubtedly an antique.

He bent to find it, swore under his breath and straightened, his face flushed. "Bloody thing can stay hiding there," he said with an attempt at humor.

"Why did you want to see me?"

Carol's quiet question washed any amusement from Keith Darcy's face. He sat down heavily. "It's about Charlotte, of course. When she's released from Naomi's clinic, will you arrest her?"

Keeping her voice soft, her tone pleasant, she

said, "The investigation isn't complete. I can't say what steps we'll be taking in the next week."

He gulped down half his drink, paused, then swallowed the remainder. "Want another? No? Well, I think I will."

With a fresh drink he sat down opposite her again and cleared his throat. "Fact is, Carol, Nora's taking this very hard . . . she's sick with worry. We all are. And Charlotte can't possibly be guilty. She couldn't — wouldn't — hurt Bryce." He paused, then said tentatively, "I'm wondering if you've considered she might have been set up by her husband . . ."

Carol rested her elbows on her chair's glossy, cold padded arms. To encourage him to talk freely she kept eye contact as she said with candor, "Officially, all I can offer you is the usual platitudes — that we're investigating every possibility, following every lead, et cetera. I do want you to know, however, that I regard the case as wide open."

"Do you know who's been drugging her?"

"Not yet. I wonder if you could make any suggestions . . ."

As he looked down at his hands, shaking his head, a voice from the doorway broke in tremulously. "Keith, why don't you say it? Why don't you tell her it's Eric?"

"Nora — what're you doing out of bed? The doctor told you to rest . . ."

Carol rose to her feet as Nora Darcy, her face haggard, walked slowly into the room. She wore a burgundy dressing gown which in other circumstances might look elegant, but the carelessly tied belt allowed it to gape open and show an expanse of nightdress. Her face was flaccid, her hair uncombed, her mouth slightly agape. As she came close to Carol she said in a slurred voice, "Keith won't say it, but I will. We think it's Eric. He's behind it all."

Keith pushed her gently into a chair, sitting on the arm and putting a protective arm around his wife's shoulders. "Inspector, Nora's not herself. She hasn't been able to sleep, so she's under medication. It makes her a little confused at times."

Making an effort to speak clearly, Nora said, "I'm not confused about Eric Higgins. Oh, he's handsome enough, and smooth too, but Bryce hated him, and with good reason."

Carol seated herself opposite the older woman and leaned forward to say gently, "Please tell me what you think."

Nora looked up at her husband, then back to Carol. "I believe, and I think Keith does too, that Eric has been drugging Charlotte." She put up a hand to forestall any response. "And don't ask me why he's been doing it . . . but with Eric there's always some angle." She shivered, pulling her dressing gown tighter around her. "That's bad enough, but I think Eric killed Bryce too."

"These are just suspicions? You have no evidence?"

Nora considered Carol's questions for so long that the tick of the ornate grandfather clock echoed in the silence. Finally she said, "He's an outsider — Eric. Never fitted in. Not like Wilma."

Keith helped his wife to her feet. "Carol, I must take her back to bed. I won't be long. Please wait — help yourself to another whiskey . . ."

Carol spent the twenty minutes he was absent

reviewing facts and considering how they fitted into various scenarios. He returned smoothing his mustache with determined strokes. Without preamble, he said, "I've decided to tell you something I consider very private. It concerns Charlotte's marriage and I'd appreciate it if it went no further than this room."

Carol achieved, she thought, the difficult task of blending encouragement and discretion in her expression.

He waited for some spoken response, but when she was silent, he continued, "Sounds bad, to put it baldly like this, but I was worried about Charlotte, so I contacted a private investigator. Only the best, of course — personally recommended to me."

"What was this private investigator to do?"

He looked surprised. "Why, to follow Eric — it was obvious something was up. I didn't want Charlotte to know anything about it — she would have been upset — so I just asked for full surveillance on her husband." With satisfaction he added, "It was expensive, but worth it. He's been seeing this woman for the past year *and* she's a psychiatric nurse, so I imagine she'd have access to drugs."

Carol said firmly, "I need full details. Everything you've got. And the name of the investigator you used."

Without a word he unlocked a drawer in the desk and took out a black vinyl folder. Handing it to her, he said, "The report's all there. Everything."

She ran her fingers down the smooth cool edge of the vinyl. "Who knows about this?"

"Only Nora and myself . . . and Bryce, I told Bryce."

"What was his reaction?"

He moved impatiently. "What would you expect? He was angry, disgusted. But he agreed with me not to say or do anything until Charlotte was better."

Gesturing with the folder, she said, "Do you think Eric Higgins suspects this exists?"

There was a pause, then he said slowly, "Only if Bryce *did* confront him . . ."

He didn't continue, but in the silence his unspoken words were almost palpable, Carol could almost hear him add, ". . . and Eric killed him."

She opened the folder. The report was extensive, with photographs and surveillance details.

"There's no doubt it's true," said Keith with grim satisfaction.

Carol closed the cover. "You asked me to keep this private, but I don't think that'll be possible. I'd like to confront Eric Higgins with this evidence."

He lifted his heavy shoulders and gave her a significant look. "I trust your discretion. I know you'll do what you can to keep things quiet."

Carol thought of Superintendent Edgar's remark that Keith Darcy and the present Minister for Police had attended the same school. His comment and look made it clear that influence was being brought to bear. He didn't need to go into detail — Carol understood perfectly.

She said, "There is one other matter I'd like to briefly discuss with you."

He looked a little surprised at her brusqueness, but indicated with a gesture that he was waiting for her questions.

"Your son's will leaves his share of Darcy Designs to his wife. Is that of any significance to the company?"

"It gives her no voting stock, if that's what you mean. Frankly, I'd buy her out, but I want to take the boys into the company as soon as they're old enough and I need to keep her on board. They have an interest of their own, of course, which I arranged when they were born."

Obviously, he considered his grandsons to be of greater value than his daughter-in-law, Carol surmised. "Your granddaughter, Megan. What's her position?"

His face softened at her name. "Next year, when Megan's twenty-five, she takes over her share of Darcy Designs stock. She's doing a business degree at present and eventually she'll take Bryce's place." He paused for effect, then said with conviction, "And when I retire, she'll run the company."

Carol said, "I understand Bryce added a codicil to his will a few months ago. It leaves some works of art — oil paintings — to his cousins . . ."

"Yes, Walter's children. Their mother, Edna, sold her interest in Darcy Designs when he died. We weren't quite as successful then as we later became, but Edna realized quite a tidy sum and moved her family to Queensland. We keep in touch, but we're not a close family."

Carol said idly, "Are the paintings valuable?"

102

Keith frowned. "I couldn't say. I have an idea Bryce bought up unknown artists he thought might later make a mark. I remember there was one oil painting that belonged in the family that Bryce particularly admired and I think Nora gave it to him as a twenty-first birthday gift. Why are you asking? Is it important?"

"Probably not." Standing, she said, "I'll be in touch when there are further developments."

He moved to touch her elbow. "Carol? he said urgently, "Nora, Charlotte — they can't take much more. I'm relying on you."

In the car on the way home, Carol expected Megan to ask questions about the meeting, but she was morose and uncommunicative. Securely belted in — a wise precaution considering Megan's precipitate driving — Carol considered Keith Darcy's final words about relying on her.

To do what? she thought sardonically. To conveniently find your son-in-law guilty?

CHAPTER SEVEN

Carol took a deep breath of the crisp air as she leaned against the lookout fence guarding the precipice. Overhead, the arching pale winter sky was streaked with mackerel clouds. Below, the huge scooped valleys released the last wisps of overnight mist to spiral lazily upward.

The Three Sisters stood impassively at Echo Point, the crumbling sandstone promontory of which their rock formation was a part etched clearly against the background of dull olive created by treetops a thousand feet below. Obeying a sudden impulse, Carol cupped her hands around her mouth and used the call that traveled so far in the loneliness of the Australian bush. "Coo-ee!" she shouted, the sound bouncing back from the weathered cliffs several times before dying away. She grinned, embarrassed. "Well, it is called Echo Point," she said.

Sybil had turned up the collar of her jacket and was rubbing her gloved hands together. "You never said it would be this cold," she said accusingly.

"So I lied to you, darling. Would I have got you out of that warm bed if I'd told you the truth?"

Marginally amused, Sybil said, "I'd be much happier there than here."

Carol started walking, saying over her shoulder, "Wait till you've stomped down a few flights over the Giant's Staircase — you'll be sweating."

Sybil rolled her eyes. "Sounds delightful. I can hardly wait."

The first metal steps began near the stone shoulder of the first Sister and were as steep as those of a ship's companionway. Sybil looked at them with unconcealed horror. "*That* goes down to the bottom of the cliff?"

Putting an arm around her, Carol said with sham solicitude, "Let me tell you the legend of the Three Sisters to take your mind off the fall below."

Sybil gave a resigned sigh. "Okay, Carol, you go first. And you can skip the legend about the three little aboriginal girls, the bunyip and the witchdoctor. Aunt Sarah gave me a blow-by-blow last night while you were out."

Carol found herself humming under her breath as they began the long descent. Her beloved Blue

Mountains, the stinging cold of the winter air and Sybil for company — the combination made her smile. She looked back to Sybil, who was frowning in concentration at each step. She wanted to say, I really do love you, but she thought about it too long and the impulse faded.

* * * * *

They arrived home at midday to Aunt Sarah's traditional Sunday dinner roast. The sizzling leg of lamb sprigged with rosemary reminded Carol of countless such winter feasts. She gazed appreciatively at her plate. The roasted vegetables — chunks of potato, triangles of pumpkin and wedges of sweet potato — were crisp on the outside, deliciously soft inside. The gravy, made with flour and the juices of the roasted meat, was complemented by Aunt Sarah's homemade mint sauce.

They ate at the big old kitchen table, Carol delighting in the warmth of affection and security that filled the room. She couldn't resist doing what she had always done as a child — squashing her peas to make a wonderful paste with gravy, potatoes and mint.

Over dessert — a golden syrup pudding that Carol couldn't resist, but could barely fit in — Sybil entertained with an exaggerated description of the horrors of their early morning hike. She was warming to the task — ". . . the stairs were bad enough, but then Carol made me hurry at this ridiculous pace around the bottom of the cliffs until we came to an elaborate torture train laughingly called the Scenic Railway. This sadistic device is designed to travel vertically up the cliff face, and, unaccountably, has no emergency resuscitation equipment on board . . ." — when someone appeared at the back door.

"Nora!" exclaimed Aunt Sarah. "Is Keith with you? If you'd been earlier you could've had lunch with us."

"No, I came over alone. I'm so sorry to interrupt you like this." Her fading fair hair was pulled smoothly back and she had applied lipstick and eye make-up. She wore golden tan slacks and an elaborate knitted sweater that featured wildflowers standing out in relief from a dark green background. Apart from her clothes, the major difference between the woman Carol had seen last night and the one who stood in the kitchen was her self-possession. Her gaze was direct and her manner resolute. She said, "Inspector — Carol — I would like to see you alone for a moment."

When they were seated in the living room, Nora said briskly, "I'm sorry about last night. Keith explained, I'm sure, that I'd taken some medication — sleeping tablets, actually. And I know he's given you the private investigator's file on Eric, but there's something he should have asked you."

Carol looked encouraging, but felt wary. She wondered if Nora was about to flex the muscle created by the Darcy name and money.

Nora leaned forward, her large hands gripping the arms of the chair. Dropping her voice, she said urgently, "Charlotte isn't guilty of Bryce's death. Please don't think anyone in the family believes she is. But at times you have to be realistic. I've no illusions about the weight of evidence you can use against her, and I'm not so naive as to think innocent people are never found guilty. What Keith wants to know . . . what I want to know . . ."

For the first time she faltered. Carol wondered if it was for effect, or if she was really hesitating to ask the bald question.

Sitting back, Nora took a deep breath then said, "Is it possible you'll charge Charlotte with manslaughter, not murder?"

"The investigation's not completed —"

"Carol, I want you to be absolutely frank with me," Nora broke in dogmatically. "If it comes to the crunch, will Charlotte be charged with murder?"

Carol felt the cold of the room settle around her as she reassessed the woman who was showing a tenacity she hadn't suspected. She replied formally. "It would depend upon your daughter's mental state — how competent she was to judge her actions at the time of your son's death. And, if it came to the worst — if Charlotte were charged with murder — your legal representatives could use experts at the committal hearing to argue that the charge be dropped to manslaughter."

Obviously exasperated by this reply, Nora shifted her large frame. "I'd like a straight answer. "Will you agree to charge Charlotte with manslaughter?"

Carol wanted to probe this militant determination. She said pleasantly, "What makes you think I'd do a deal with you, here, in private?"

"A deal?" Nora's lips tightened. "I'm asking for consideration, not a deal. And I can't see it presents you with any problem, Carol. It's obvious Charlotte's been badly affected by drugs. Drugs, I must

108

emphasize, she didn't know she was taking. If —
and it's a big if — Charlotte had anything to do
with what happened, she can't possibly have been in
any state to know what was going on." She stood,
looking down frostily from her considerable height.
"And why haven't you arrested Eric? It's perfectly
obvious he and his lover have been working together
against Charlotte."

To take back the advantage, Carol also rose, but
still had to tilt her head to meet Nora's flat stare.
"It's a matter of evidence. We can't arrest someone
on suspicion alone."

"Then what are you doing here at Sarah's?"
asked Nora acidly. "I imagine your time would be
better served gathering the required evidence, don't
you?"

She seemed taken aback at Carol's reply, which
was delivered with a faint smile. "But that's what
I'm doing here, of course."

* * * * *

Nora refused Aunt Sarah's invitation to stay, and
Sybil announced she had to lie down to recover from
the rigors of the morning, so Carol had the
opportunity to combine washing the dinner dishes
with pumping her aunt for background information.
"Tell me about Nora and Keith . . . who's the
driving force in the marriage?"

Aunt Sarah, tea towel at the ready, closely
inspected a plate Carol had just washed. "Well,
everybody'd say Keith, of course. He's got the
business brains and he's made Darcy Designs into a
huge success. Nora's a manipulator, though. Always

109

got her own way, but usually doesn't let her claws show. It was the same even when she was drinking heavily. She wraps it up as gentle persuasion, but she can make anyone jump if she puts her mind to it . . . Keith, Bryce, Charlotte — they all listen to her. Mind, the one who *can* stand up to her is Megan."

"What about Bryce's wife?"

"Wilma? There's a bit of an unholy alliance there. Nora was determined Bryce would marry. During the engagement he got cold feet. She worked with Wilma to make sure he carried it through."

"So Nora and Wilma are friends?"

Aunt Sarah sniffed at the word. "Not exactly friends . . . more allies, dear. United in their life's work — to control their men through a nice combination of persuasion and threats. Of course, you haven't seen either of them in a situation where they don't get their own way. Different methods, but both quite capable of making life hell for everyone until they get what they want. Keith and Bryce both found it easier to give in than put up with it."

"Can you imagine either of them being upset enough to physically attack Bryce?"

Aunt Sarah made a face. "You're thinking his death's a temper tantrum gone dreadfully wrong?"

Carol handed her another plate. "Just trying out some ideas, Aunt."

"Wash this one again."

"What's wrong with it?"

Aunt Sarah pointed out a speck. "Right there. Suppose you use a dishwasher at home, eh?" Watching Carol plunge the offending plate back into the suds, she said, "I've known Nora more years than I care to count. Seen her in some wicked rages when she was younger. But after she married Keith she calmed down . . . you'd see the fire in her eyes, but she kept it under control. As for Wilma, she can be snappy, bad-tempered, but that's all. She's not the type to fly off the handle — it might put her at a disadvantage."

Carol dubiously eyed the congealed gravy in the baking dish. She said, "Was Nora upset when Charlotte took over most of the design work for the company?"

"Not that you'd notice. Of course, it didn't happen overnight. It was a gradual thing, started with the first of the spells Nora took in Naomi Reed's clinic. Don't think it sank in for a while — what was happening, I mean."

"So Charlotte now does nearly all the design work for the company?"

"It's more than that," said her aunt positively, "As far as the creative side is concerned, Charlotte *is* Darcy Designs." She gave a critical look at the clean baking dish Carol handed her as she added, "And that's why her behavior lately and now this situation are such a disaster. She's halfway through a new batch of designs for next season."

"Could Nora step in?"

Aunt Sarah began to assault every flat surface in sight with a damp dishcloth. "Frankly," she said, "I'd say Nora'd be a bit rusty. No one at Darcy Designs wants Charlotte in jail — they'll do anything to make sure she isn't put there."

The phone rang. Aunt Sarah snatched it up with a wet hand, then handed the damp receiver to Carol. "It's your Mark Bourke."

111

Carol, aware that her aunt was listening avidly, was carefully noncommittal in her replies to Bourke's information. "Would you have Wilma Darcy's telephone number? Thought I'd see her while I'm here."

Aunt Sarah frowned her displeasure. "First you talk to Sergeant Bourke late last night, then he calls you back today. I don't suppose you're going to give me a hint about what's going on?"

Carol could imagine her aunt's reaction if she was told that Darcy's wife had lied about her whereabouts when her husband had died. "Official business, Aunt Sarah," she said chidingly. "So how could you even ask?"

* * * * *

Bryce and Wilma's house was in a favored part of Katoomba with sweeping views of Megalong Valley, which formed part of the Blue Mountains National Park. The building seemed to grow out of the exposed rocks on which it was set, its wooden walls stained in harmony with the warm sandstone. The landscaping was subtle, with native plants and trees giving an effect of natural, if disciplined, bushland.

Now this, Carol thought approvingly, is much more in sympathy with the surroundings than the monstrosity I saw last night. She had turned on the wide wooden steps to admire the view when the front door opened.

"You'd better come in," said Wilma Darcy without enthusiasm, her full red mouth tight. She was wearing snugly cut beige pants with a matching jacket and light tan boots with very high heels. She shut the door behind Carol with more force than necessary and led the way down the hall, her heels beating an emphatic tattoo as she walked.

It was obvious to Carol that the room Wilma entered had been designed with children in mind. Bright and basic colors, the surfaces easy to clean, and there were no vases or knickknacks to be knocked over by enthusiastic little bodies. The couches and chairs were covered with multi-patterned material, two mini-desks with matching chairs sat side by side, and several painted chests, one of which was open, spilled toys and games onto the floor.

A girl about fifteen got to her feet as they came into the room. She had been sitting on the rug helping the two young blond-headed boys to do a jumbo jigsaw puzzle.

Wilma didn't introduce Carol. Instead she said to the girl as she handed her money, "Lisa, use as much of this as you need. If you leave now you'll get there well before the movie starts."

Carol was ignored as the next few minutes were taken up with the putting on of coats, admonishments to the boys to behave and instructions of exactly what they were permitted to eat during the intermission.

Wilma went to see them off, then returned to Carol with a mutinous expression on her face. "I don't expect to be interrupted this way during the weekend, but I'm hardly surprised. My sister, Darlene, called me after Sergeant Bourke gave her the third degree."

Carol said politely, "Do you mind if I sit down?"

Wilma gestured vaguely in the direction of a couch, then lowered herself into a deep chair. She surveyed Carol's casual clothes with a faint expression of disdain. Finally she said, "This anonymous call that sent you to my sister — the person knew why I'd gone down to Sydney?"

"The information was that you had been in Sydney last Monday, not, as you had said in your statement, home here in the Blue Mountains. Mention was made of your car being parked outside your sister's place during the afternoon."

Wilma said with sudden intensity, "Was it a man or a woman?"

"Almost certainly a woman," said Carol, interested to see her reaction.

Wilma gave a slight nod, almost as if she was satisfied with this information. Carol said, "Do you have any idea who the woman might be?"

Wilma checked her fingernails. "Not really," she said.

Carol said bluntly, "Someone tries to incriminate you in your husband's murder and you're not very interested?"

"I had nothing to do with Bryce's death! I can't understand why you're asking these questions when you've got Charlotte — she was *there* with his body. Isn't that enough for you?"

"Have you heard the name Janice Russo?"

Carol's sudden question made Wilma look at her directly. "No, never," she said, her self-possession regained.

Although not sure whether Wilma's answer was true, Carol didn't pursue the issue. Instead, wanting to jolt the woman's composure, she said accusingly,

"You lied about where you were when your husband was murdered."

"Why can't I have any privacy?" asked Wilma in a shaking, throaty voice, as she covered her face with her hands.

As Carol let the silence lengthen, she noted the many rings Wilma wore, the largest of which, a diamond and ruby engagement ring, was almost gaudy in its size and setting.

At last Wilma raised her head, her large gray eyes quite dry. She said with a slight tremor, "My marriage wasn't entirely happy . . . nothing serious, juts a bit of friction. I didn't want anyone here to know there was trouble between us, so I secretly arranged to see a marriage guidance counselor in Sydney. Of course, my sister knew all about it — the counselor was someone she'd seen too." She stopped for a moment to extract a lace handkerchief and dab at her eyes. "Bryce wouldn't agree to be involved, so I went alone. I arranged with Lisa to pick up Jill's children and my boys after school in a taxi. And she stayed here and minded them until I got home late in the afternoon."

"I need the full details so your story can be checked out." Wilma turned her face away and rested her forehead on one hand. Irritated by what seemed a try for sympathy, Carol said firmly, "You lied. Why?"

Wilma's look was a plea for understanding, "I was so shocked at what had happened. I wasn't thinking straight and it seemed easier just to let you think I was here."'

Raising her eyebrows, Carol said with a hint of astonishment, "You were told that your husband had been murdered, and you immediately thought of what would be easier for you — what you could get away with?"

Wilma's lips trembled. "I had nothing to do with Bryce being killed and I didn't want anyone to know I'd been to counseling — people gossip and I particularly didn't want his family involved. The best thing to do, I thought, was to say I had a day like any other day."

"So you were with someone who can vouch for you every minute between two and three o'clock on Monday afternoon?" As Wilma hesitated, Carol added, "Your sister's statement makes it clear you weren't with her at that time."

Wilma twisted her handkerchief in anxious hands. "Inspector, surely you don't think I'd lie again?"

Of course you would, if you thought you could get away with it, thought Carol. She said, "I must ask you to come with me to the local police station where you can make an accurate statement." She was sure the slight emphasis on the second last word would not be lost on Wilma, however upset she might appear to be.

CHAPTER EIGHT

The bleak Monday afternoon was drawing to a premature close as heavy clouds raced to extinguish the last rays of the sun. Carol and Bourke watched Janice Russo park her car and enter the building. They gave her a few minutes, then followed. As they walked up the worn carpeting of the stairs to the apartment, Bourke said, "Ran a check on Eric Higgins' past business experience. Has a record of starting small companies that do okay for a while, then fall to pieces. Seems he gets too ambitious too soon, never has enough capital to cover his grandiose ideas. His first wife — she died of cancer before he met Charlotte Darcy — bankrolled him in two businesses, both of which went bust."

"You think the Darcy money attracted him?"

"Well, it wouldn't hurt . . . and he wasn't to know the family controlled funds so tightly. Probably thought by marrying Charlotte he'd secure an endless line of credit."

Carol assessed Janice Russo as Bourke explained their presence on her doorstep. She wasn't conventionally pretty, but her looks were arresting. She had thick, straight brown hair framing a face with almost Slavic lines — the cheekbones high, the jaw strong, the eyes subtly slanted and dark. Her mouth was wide, thin-lipped, mobile, with small, even teeth. She was wearing a slightly grubby nurse's uniform a little tight across the breast and short enough to give a generous view of her shapely thighs.

Leaning against the doorjamb, arms folded, she showed every evidence of impatience. Finally she interrupted Bourke's explanations. "Look, I'm not trying to hide the fact that Eric's a friend of mine," she said in a high nasal twang, "but I've never met Bryce Darcy in my life. I've just got off duty, right? I'm tired and I don't have to answer your questions anyway, do I?"

She gave a contemptuous laugh when Bourke suggested the alternative of accompanying them to the local police station for a formal interview. "I didn't come down in the last shower — I know my rights. I don't have to ask you in. I don't have to answer any questions."

Carol said conversationally, "The situation changes somewhat, Ms Russo, should we come to the conclusion you're involved in some material way."

Janice Russo straightened, unfolded her arms, tilted her head back and looked at Carol, her glance flickering over Carol's bottle-green suit, white silk blouse and discreet jewelry. "So you're the famous Detective Inspector Carol Ashton — I've seen you on television often enough. The Darcy family wheeled you in to clean up the mess, have they?

Carol said mildly, "You think the Darcys have that much influence?"

"Money buys everything."

Intrigued by the bitterness of the reply, Carol said, "We're investigating Bryce Darcy's murder. It's just another case. Money doesn't make any difference."

At the word murder Carol noticed a subtle change come over Janice Russo. She looked away from Carol to the floor, her face showing for a moment a shadow of uncertainty.

Bourke had seen it too. He said smoothly, "A few questions now may be all we need, then we won't bother you again."

"All right," she said ungraciously, standing aside to allow them to enter. "But if this gets heavy, I'm shutting up and getting legal advice. Understand that."

With a negligent gesture she indicated they were to find somewhere to sit. Her flat was small and sparsely furnished, but each item, Carol decided, had been carefully chosen by someone with a taste for quality. Becoming aware that Janice Russo was

119

watching her inspection with hostility, Carol smiled. "A Margaret Preston, isn't it?" she said, indicating a delicate etching of flowers.

"Yes. I didn't know cops had such good taste."

Ignoring her derision Carol said, "We've told you we're investigating Bryce Darcy's murder —"

Moving uneasily in her chair, Janice said, "I don't know anything about it. I told you, I never even met the guy."

She's more than anxious, Carol thought. She's frightened. She said pleasantly, "Then perhaps you know his wife, Wilma Darcy?"

"His wife? Why in the hell would I know her?"

Carol looked at her in slight surprise. "Well, it seems she's familiar with your name."

Truculent, Janice threw back her head. "Look, I don't know her. Never met her, *or* her husband. Okay?"

Letting the silence last for a while, Carol finally said, "But you do know Eric Higgins well. Very well, in fact."

"So what if I do?"

Bourke riffled through his notebook. He said, "Is it true that you've been on intimate terms with Mr. Higgins for the past year?"

Janice snorted. "Intimate terms?" she said scornfully. "If you mean are we lovers, the answer's yes — not that it's any business of yours." She frowned. "How did you know about it? We were bloody careful . . ."

Bourke flipped over another page of his notebook. "Perhaps Mrs. Darcy's brother was aware of your relationship with his sister's husband."

Carol saw her jaw tighten, but she said offhandedly, "I wouldn't know."

Bourke smiled, all friendly interest. "How about the future? Are you and Mr. Higgins planning to marry?"

Janice Russo considered this question warily. At last she said, "I can't see that's any of your business."

"But it is, I'm afraid," said Carol. With a hint of silky menace she continued, "If Eric Higgins intended to become financially secure before he broke up his marriage, then the fact that his brother-in-law knew about *you* becomes extremely important."

"Someone murdered Bryce Darcy for a reason," added Bourke helpfully.

"So why haven't you arrested his sister? She was found with her brother's body, wasn't she? The family paying you to find someone else to blame, are they?"

Ignoring her questions, Bourke said, "Charlotte Darcy has been admitted to a clinic suffering from amphetamine intoxication."

She looked at him blankly, but Carol saw her knuckles whiten as she clenched her hands. "So? What's it to me?"

Bourke raised his eyebrows slightly. "As a psychiatric nurse, I imagine you'd have access to drugs, including amphetamines."

"Everything's controlled, signed for."

He continued, "And you'd know the details, the dosage, how to administer it, the effects it would have . . ."

She glared defiantly. "I don't know what you're getting at."

Carol said, "Let's look at a hypothetical situation, Ms Russo. A person is secretly dosed with considerable quantities of amphetamines and as a consequence becomes irrational and possibly dangerous to herself and to other people. While under the influence of these drugs, she commits a murder." She paused for a moment. "Do you understand the law in this state regarding accessories before and after the fact?"

Janice Russo licked her lips. "This is nothing to do with me."

Bourke said meditatively, "You know, the full weight of the law can fall upon an accessory to murder . . ."

"I tell you, it's nothing to do with me!"

"In effect," said Bourke, "it's as though the accessory himself — or herself — committed the murder."

Bourke's final words brought an immediate response. Janice Russo stood, agitated. "Oh, no, you're not going to land me with that! I had nothing to do with feeding her drugs."

Carol and Bourke remained seated. To press the advantage, Carol said deliberately, "We believe you were directly involved in a systematic attempt to poison Charlotte Darcy with amphetamines."

"Poison her? I'm not going to be lumbered with something I didn't do." She stared at Carol, her manner a mixture of defiance and fear. "Go on and check the hospital drug records. You'll see there's nothing missing. You've got no right to accuse me of anything."

Carol glanced at Bourke, who said, "And then, Ms Russo, there's the matter of Bryce Darcy's murder . . ."

Her belligerence draining away, Janice sat down. "I've got nothing to do with murder."

Carol said smoothly, "Perhaps not with murder, but how about drugging Charlotte Darcy?"

"I told him it was a bloody stupid idea."

"You're trying to tell us it was all Eric Higgins?" Bourke sounded surprised. "Nothing at all to do with you?"

She was anxious to explain. "Yes, it was Eric — all his idea. You can't blame me. Honest, he went on and on about drugs . . ."

"Let's get this straight," said Bourke. "Eric Higgins explained the effect he wanted, and you advised him on the drug to use. Have I got it right?"

Looking ill, Janice said, "All I did was discuss it. I never got him any drugs. Not once."

Carol thought of the terror and confusion Charlotte Darcy had endured. She said with a trace of contempt, "You gave Eric Higgins detailed information about dosages and effects of amphetamines, knowing all the time he was intending to give them to his wife."

Janice looked at her appealingly. "It's not as bad as that, truly. Actually I tried to stop him, but he wouldn't listen. It was one of his harebrained schemes. At first I went along with it for a laugh. Honest, I couldn't believe he was serious."

"What was this scheme of his?" asked Bourke.

"He said Charlotte wouldn't give him enough money to really get his business on a sound footing.

In fact, he said Bryce was trying to persuade his sister to stop giving him anything at all. Eric was really upset. He told me he just needed some capital and a bit more time, and the video business would be booming."

Bourke said, "Why didn't he try to raise the money elsewhere?"

Janice looked both angry and defensive. "Well, why would he? The Darcys have plenty and it wouldn't have hurt them to give him a few hundred thousand."

"Did *you* give him any money?" asked Bourke.

"Me?" she said bitterly. "If I had any to spare do you think I'd be living in this dump?" She gestured impatiently. "Like I said, Eric needed money badly. A couple of years ago Eric's sister had a serious mental breakdown. She's never married and there was no one to look after her affairs. A court gave Eric power of attorney so he could pay her bills, operate her accounts, that sort of thing. It was only temporary — when his sister recovered the power of attorney was canceled. He told me about it and he starting joking about getting the same arrangement over Charlotte's affairs so he could fix his business without interference." She leaned forward persuasively. "I thought he was joking, honest I did. Then after a while I could see he wasn't joking any more. He was seriously trying to find a way to do it."

"And you helped him."

Janice winced at Carol's accusing tone. "It wasn't my fault, I tell you. He already knew what overdoses of drugs could do — I often talked about my work, didn't I — and then he came up with his idea that his wife could have a breakdown . . ."

Carol was sure the pause was to assess their response, so she said briskly, "Are you saying that Eric Higgins intended to have his wife committed?"

"Well, yes. Eric thought that if he could get Charlotte behaving irrationally — and he said he knew this psychiatrist who'd be easy to persuade she was unbalanced — then he'd engineer a similar arrangement to the one he had with his sister. With power of attorney he'd be able to get to Charlotte's private accounts. He swore it wouldn't be a long-term thing . . . just time enough to build up his video business, so that when Charlotte came good again, she'd keep on investing because she'd see what a success it could be."

Bourke was incredulous. "And he thought this was a possibility? He wouldn't have any trouble convincing a court his wife was off her head?"

Janice Russo looked both sulky and apprehensive. "I told him it wouldn't work, but he went ahead anyway. It wasn't anything to do with me, honest."

"But Ms Russo," said Carol coldly, "it's clear that you are very much involved. Certainly you did nothing to stop what was happening." Visualizing Charlotte Darcy's ravaged face as she had last seen it, she added curtly, "Sergeant Bourke will caution you. Perhaps you'd like to change clothes before you come with us to make a full statement."

* * * * *

125

"Pick up Eric Higgins?" said Bourke outside the interrogation room where Janice Russo was reading through a typed copy of her statement.

Carol considered the options. "Why not send out Anne Newsome to invite him in for a chat?"

He nodded. "Do you want to do the interview?"

Carol, feeling altruistic, said, "I might look in, but why don't you and Anne handle it. You're always saying she needs the experience."

Bourke smiled slightly. "Are you sure Constable Newsome's up to the responsibility? This is an important one and you won't be happy, Carol, if something goes wrong."

Remembering the excitement of the first big case she'd had, the first time she'd been trusted to strategize an interview, to question a major suspect, Carol said, "Come on Mark, you've spent a lot of time telling me how good she is. Have you changed your mind?"

"No, I haven't." He paused, decided to say something more. "Carol, I'll give her a go on this one, but I want you to remember what it was like when you were in her position."

Puzzled, Carol said, "What's my early career got to do with it?"

"I don't want you being too hard on Anne." As she frowned, he added, "You don't take kindly to mistakes — and you can be rough, Carol, with the things you say."

Carol passed his comment off with a smile. "I'll be nice," she said flippantly, "and I'll leave Eric Higgins to you and Anne."

But under her light words she felt defensive and hurt at his unaccustomed criticism.

* * * * *

Carol came into Eric Higgins' interview well after it had started. The room, with its bare walls, anonymous furniture and glaring overhead lighting seemed too small and insignificant for Eric Higgins' handsome presence. He lounged at apparent ease, his hands in the pockets of his dark gray slacks, his blue cashmere sweater intensifying the color of his eyes.

As Carol entered he straightened in his chair, smoothed back his black hair, essayed a smile. "Inspector Ashton! You've come to conduct the interview, I hope. I don't want too late a night . . ."

It occurred to Carol how accustomed he must be to using his looks to gain him favor. She was disconcerted at her next thought: *As I am.*

She glanced at Anne Newsome who was sitting tensely at the other end of the table, several unopened folders in front of her. Bourke, in shirtsleeves, had positioned himself to one side, his chair pushed a little back, his expression one of mild interest.

Carol said, "I'm just here to listen to your replies, Mr. Higgins."

His black eyebrows drew down. "But surely . . ."

Carol ignored him, gave a slight nod to indicate Anne should continue, and seated herself outside his immediate field of vision; to see her he would have to turn his head. This would make it more difficult for him to try to include her in the interview.

Higgins attempted to negate this by swinging his chair half around as he said, "Inspector, I've been telling your colleagues that I have absolutely no idea

127

where Charlotte got amphetamines. If you asked for my opinion, off the record, naturally, I'd say her daughter's the source. After all, she *is* a university student, and drugs of all sorts would be easy for her to get."

Carol didn't respond. Anne Newsome caught his attention with two words.

He turned back to her, too quickly. "What did you say?"

"I said, Janice Russo."

He put his elbows on the table, linked his fingers. "Is there an ashtray?" he said.

Bourke leaned over and placed in front of him a dented metal dish, marked with the deaths of countless cigarettes. Higgins felt in his pockets, bringing out a flat metal cigarette case and an elegant gold lighter. He selected a cigarette, tapped it on the case with slightly trembling fingers, then lit it with careful precision. Blowing out a stream of smoke, he said, "Don't use these much these days." His glance flickered over Anne and Bourke, then he turned and looked at Carol. "Can I offer you a cigarette, Inspector?"

She shook her head. Anne said, "Do you know a Janice Russo?"

Higgins examined his cigarette closely. At last he said, "I can't see what this has to do with Charlotte."

Carol thought, you really are so good-looking. And you still think there's some way you'll charm your way out of this.

Her gaze shifted to Anne Newsome. Why am I resenting you so much? she silently asked, although she already knew he answer. It was because she felt supplanted. She, herself, wanted to take over the questioning, working in the easy, familiar partnership with Mark that they had developed over the years. She wanted to be in for the kill, to nail the man who sat there prevaricating, thinking he could wriggle out of accountability for what he had done.

Bourke said, "We have a statement from Ms Russo."

Higgins drew hard on the cigarette. He leaned forward with every evidence of frankness. "I do know Janice," he said to Bourke, his soft, rich tones implying that he was making quite a concession to admit it. He added casually, "How did you get her name?"

Bourke didn't respond and Anne regained Eric Higgins' attention with her next words, "You and Janice Russo have been lovers for over a year."

"Did *she* say that?"

Bourke smiled. "What do *you* say, Mr. Higgins?"

It was an old trick, to switch from questioner to questioner, so that the person couldn't settle, couldn't form that ephemeral relationship that could occur between two people during an interrogation. Carol was tempted to make it a three-way questioning, but then remembered her earlier promise to Bourke.

It was Anne's turn. "Are you denying the relationship?"

"I don't deny we're friends. I would like to know who told you about us."

Bourke leaned back, putting his hands behind his head. "Close friends?" he asked.

"I suppose so." Higgins stubbed out his cigarette nonchalantly. "Will this take much longer?"

"In fact," said Anne, "you have a sexual relationship with Janice Russo, don't you?"

Higgins grinned, spread his hands in a gesture of defeat, said, "You've got me. I'm not proud of it, but yes, Janice and I are lovers. I won't bore you with any comments about my marriage, but . . ." He paused, apparently to allow his audience to guess at the shortcomings of his union with Charlotte Darcy.

He turned to Carol. "Inspector, Charlotte would be upset if she knew . . . I wonder if this can remain confidential?"

Bourke stood, pushing his chair back with a grating sound. He paced around the room, hands in his pockets, eyes fixed on Eric Higgins. "We're not interested in your sex life as such — that's your business. This investigation concerns Bryce Darcy's murder." He took his hands out of his pockets and leaned over the table to enumerate points on his fingers. "First, your brother-in-law was battered to death on your property between two and three o'clock last Monday afternoon. Second, you had time between business appointments to return home. Third, Bryce certainly knew about your affair with Janice Russo."

"He couldn't have known!"

Picking up a black folder from the table, Bourke said, "Bryce Darcy read this, Mr. Higgins. It's a report — a very detailed report — of your activities with Janice Russo."

Higgins fumbled with his cigarette case. "Bryce put a private eye on me, did he?" He tapped the cigarette irritably, then said with deep sincerity, "He might have known about Janice, but he never said anything to me." He looked up suddenly, as if struck with a thought, "He must've told Charlotte . . ."

Carol was sure he had paused to allow them all to consider Charlotte's guilt. She saw the contempt she felt for his blatant attempt to set up his wife mirrored on Anne Newsome's face, but none of this was reflected in Anne's voice as she said conversationally, "Are you saying that you believe your wife killed her brother because he told her you were having an affair?"

He made an open-handed, trust-me gesture. "It's possible . . . I'm not saying it's true . . . but you know Charlotte had an overdose of amphetamines. I don't want to believe it, but she might have been so upset . . ."

Bourke sounded bored. "Janice says you got the amphetamines in powder form from a dealer at Kings Cross, then you substituted capsules filled with the drug for the vitamin capsules you'd persuaded your wife to take. She also says you tried dissolving the powder in orange juice to disguise its bitter taste."

Higgins' face glistened with beads of sweat. He wiped his fingers along his upper lip, then said, "I have a right to make a phone call. I want legal representation before I answer any more questions."

"You've been watching too many American movies," said Bourke cheerfully. "In New South Wales you don't have any particular legal right to use the telephone. However, under the circumstances, Constable Newsome will be glad to contact anyone you nominate."

Catching Bourke's glance, Carol gestured that she

wanted to speak to him outside. He followed her, closed the door firmly on Eric Higgins and Anne Newsome, and said, "She's doing okay, Carol."

Carol nodded agreement. "Mark, this is going to be a long hard haul. He'll hold out as long as he can, then he'll admit drugging his wife because it's the lesser of two evils — he doesn't want to run any chance of being charged with murder."

Bourke rubbed his hand over his chin. "What're your instincts, Carol? You think he might have killed Bryce to shut him up about Janice Russo?"

"Money's a better motive. If Bryce stops funds going into Charlotte's accounts then Higgins has much less to play with if he does manage to get power of attorney."

Bourke shook his head. "I don't think he has the guts to commit murder. He's a dreamer. He'd come up with some complicated way of getting rid of his brother-in-law, but he'd never carry it through."

"Complicated?" said Carol. "Surely drugging your wife and then setting her up for a murder charge is complicated enough, even for Eric Higgins."

CHAPTER NINE

Carol smiled at the cats as they played an elaborate game of hide and seek around the furniture. Shortly the lure of the fire would mean a truce from mock hostilities so that they could curl themselves in neat packages by its radiant heat.

Sybil handed her a whiskey and sank down on the sofa beside her. "Carol, are you still thinking of resigning?"

Carol sighed. "I don't know, darling. I'm tired of the system, the political influence, the importance of who you know rather than what you know."

"Is it as bad as all that?"

Aware that her bleak outlook tended to exaggerate the negative and ignore the positive, she sighed again and said, "Probably not, but I look at someone like Anne Newsome at the beginning of her career — bright, eager — and I wonder how she's going to take the inevitable compromises, the subtle pressures, not to mention the sheer bloody grind of police work."

"Seems to me," said Sybil lightly, "that you're just a little jaundiced. Maybe you need a vacation."

"Perhaps I need a permanent holiday from the Force."

The words, spoken, seemed to Carol too definitive, too final.

Suddenly serious, Sybil said, "Have you thought it through? Have you considered what you might do?"

Carol stared moodily at her drink, clinking the ice against the sides of the glass. "What's an ex-cop fit for? Security work? Joining the ranks of the private investigators?"

"Madeline Shipley offered you work in television. You know you could always go in that direction."

"If I take that option I'd better hurry," said Carol, determined to be morose. "If you're a woman you don't last once your looks start to go."

This drew a mocking snort from Sybil. "And you're crumbling fast, Carol. You might consider plastic surgery to stave off the inevitable collapse."

Carol smiled unwillingly. "I'm being impossible, I know. It's just that I don't feel like playing the game any more. I used to enjoy it — putting everything together, solving the puzzle, making the case watertight. Now . . ."

"Now?"

Carol took a swallow of her drink. "Part of it is Vicki," she admitted reluctantly. "She's so sure, so certain. If she were gay, I can't imagine her hiding it for an instant."

"Don't be so sure. Like anybody else, Vicki's got her blind spots, and one of them's a total conviction that her view of the world is the only valid one. Put her in your shoes, in your position, and things wouldn't look quite the same."

Carol raised an eyebrow. "I don't remember you criticizing Vicki before."

"It's so easy to get swept up in her enthusiasm — and she does so much good. Women's groups need dynamos like Vicki to push everyone to the limit, to make impossible things possible. And without her I wouldn't have been so involved in the education of exploited migrant women. Now, I really feel I'm doing something that makes a real difference to people's lives . . . not just the women, but their children and families as well. And all that's due to Vicki Thorpe, activist with a capital A."

Carol made a face. "She'd be exhausting to live with."

"You wouldn't live with Vicki," Sybil laughed. "You'd just hover on the periphery, vaguely waving as she hurtles by."

* * * * *

Sybil was cleaning her teeth while Carol showered. Handing Carol a towel, she said, "Would you do something for me tonight?"

"Sure. What is it?"

"I mean in bed." At Carol's anticipatory smile, Sybil added, "You may not like it."

"Leather? Whips? Bondage?" said Carol, highly amused. "Or do you want me to dress as a schoolgirl?"

"I want you to do absolutely nothing. I want you to leave it all to me."

Carol knew her expression had changed. Sybil said, "I said you mightn't like it."

Carol felt oddly defensive. "It's just that I . . ." She shrugged to complete the sentence.

"Humor me?"

This is ridiculous, thought Carol, realizing that she was apprehensive. She was used to dominance, to being in control. Even when Sybil was the initiator, Carol could command her own response, direct their love-making, maintain authority.

"Carol?"

After all, this is the woman I love, thought Carol. Aloud she said firmly, "You've got a deal."

Wrapping the towel around her, she followed Sybil into the bedroom, admiring the line of her back, her buttocks, the slim elegance of her wrists. "Am I allowed to do anything at all?" she asked as they got into bed.

"No."

"And how do you want me? Lying on my back — my stomach — lotus position . . . ?" She had to smile at the resignation in her own voice.

Sybil had become serious, concentrated, her voice a husky whisper. "Just let me love you."

The bedside lamp threw a soft circle of light on the ceiling. Carol, submitting, tried to make Sybil smile by saying in jest, "Please — you will be gentle, won't you?"

"No conversation," said Sybil, kissing the corner of her mouth.

Sybil's touch was soft, persistent, maddening. She stroked Carol's skin, massaged her feet, ran fingers down her arms, her thighs. But never enough, never reaching her nipples or the cleft between her legs. And then she began to kiss her, lips sliding over her still slightly damp skin, nibbling her ear lobes, licking the hollow at the base of her neck, gently biting her shoulders.

Carol wanted to seize Sybil's head in her two hands to force her to take a hardening nipple into her mouth, but instead she lay inert, arms by her sides, pulse quickening, the muscles in her back tensing, her hips beginning to lift of their own accord.

This is agony, she thought. And then — sweet agony. A sensuous, slow, spiraling excitement was building in her. Not in bright colors, not yet, but in patterns and shades, in soft whispers.

She heard herself gasp, groan. A delicate, insistent fire had begun to consume her, running its demanding warmth in tremors, in waves, in tides throughout her body. And as she surrendered, as she gave herself up to its tender urgency, the warmth grew to a molten, exacting force.

It was slipping away, her command, her

authority. All that was left in her consciousness was liquid flame filling her to overflowing, lifting her to a roaring silence where her body existed only as a conflagration of desire.

And at the same time she was aware of Sybil, of her breath now delicate against her thighs, her tongue searching and finding the opening wetness. Distantly, she could hear herself calling out, but she couldn't make words from the sounds.

She was transcending physical need, pushing against the barriers that held her heart and spirit. For a moment — one pulsing, vivid moment — she saw, felt, understood. Then she was part of the joyous breaking waves of orgasm, her mind bursting into splintered fragments, obliterating the insight she had overleapt her body to achieve.

Again and again, wild with ecstasy, riding the rolling breakers into the safe haven of Sybil's arms.

CHAPTER TEN

Carol had arranged for Megan Darcy to come into her office first thing on Tuesday morning. She arrived half an hour after the designated time.

"Sorry I'm late," she said without any indication of regret, adding defiantly, "I don't know why you need to see me anyway."

Carol didn't waste time with preliminaries. "You made an anonymous call to say that Wilma Darcy was in Sydney on Monday when she claimed to be in Katoomba."

Megan lounged in the chair, her hands shoved

into the pockets of her well-worn jeans. She wore a red and white checked sweatshirt and a hostile expression. Her dark eyes fixed on Carol, she said, "I don't have any idea what you're talking about."

Carol smiled her disbelief.

Chin lifted, Megan kept eye contact, finally saying, "Anyhow, she *was* in Sydney, wasn't she?"

"You know she was. What I'm interested in is how you knew."

The trace of urgency in Carol's tone was not lost on Megan. "Why is it important?" she demanded.

"I don't know if it is," said Carol frankly. She looked at Megan with sympathy, thinking of the effect the murder of her uncle and the possible arrest of her mother must be having upon her.

Megan shifted under her gaze, apparently disconcerted by its compassion. "Look," she said, "I didn't want to get involved in a slanging match with Wilma. It was easier to just call and give the information."

"How did you know she'd lied?"

"I saw Wilma's car parked outside her sister's place on Monday morning."

Apparently considering this explanation enough, Megan took her hands out of her pockets and sat up straight as if preparing to leave.

Carol shook her head gently. "That's not good enough, Megan. You just happened to be driving through Parramatta and by chance saw her car . . . ?"

Slumping back in the chair, Megan said, "Oh, all right! I didn't see her car — I didn't need to. She always goes to Darlene's place and bitches on about the Darcy family. She's greedy, you know. She's got a lot, and she wants more. And she knows Grandfather favors me, so she can't stand me —"

"How did you know she was in Sydney?" repeated Carol implacably.

"Uncle Bryce told me. He called me on Sunday to ask how Mum was because he was coming down to see her on Monday. And he told me Wilma had tried to get him to go to a marriage guidance counselor the next day with her, and he'd refused, but she was going ahead with the appointment anyway."

Carol began to feel a tingle of anticipation. The pieces were beginning to fit together, not yet in any coherent picture, but tantalizing close to recognizable shapes.

As she sat looking at Megan Darcy, she had a flash of insight. The drive that had always impelled her towards the solving of puzzles, the investigation of criminal cause and effect, was not, as she had always believed, a combination of the excitement of the chase and the satisfaction of solving problems. It was much more. To plumb the mystery at the center of each person — their secret thoughts and motivations, the enigma that was the core of their personalities — this had given her the deepest and most satisfying reward.

She picked up her gold pen and began to turn it over in her fingers. "Do you know why Wilma thought it necessary to see a counselor?"

Megan had obviously made a decision to cooperate. Her tone was close to contrite as she said, "I should've come to you before, Inspector, but I didn't want to think it was important. I don't know anything about Wilma and the counselor she was going to, but I do know that Uncle Bryce had an appointment to see a psychiatrist on Monday morning."

"Naomi Reed?" said Carol, quickly.

"No, it definitely wasn't her, because he would have said so. I got the impression it was a man, but I don't know his name. Uncle Bryce made a joke about it, but he sounded unhappy. I couldn't work out why he was telling me, and just when I thought he was going to explain, he sort of stopped, and changed the subject."

Carol's further questions elicited no further information, and as she stood to close the interview, Megan said urgently, "Inspector, before I go . . . My mother . . . Do you think she killed Uncle Bryce?"

With a thrill of certainty, based neither upon intuition nor sympathy, Carol knew that Charlotte Darcy was innocent. Unable to say this officially, she said with genuine regret, "I'm sorry, I can't comment."

* * * * *

Carol sat reading the statements made by Janice Russo and Eric Higgins the night before. Higgins had been charged with administering a deleterious substance to his wife, had spent the night in the cells and was appearing before a magistrate for a bail hearing that morning. Bourke had released Janice Russo with the proviso that she remain available for further possible charges. As he handed Carol the statements, Bourke had said to her, "I left the two of them with the strongest impression that I was hoping to nail them for the rather more serious crime of murder, but if all else failed, slow poisoning

142

by amphetamine overdose should be worth a year or two."

She was smiling wryly at Janice and Eric's attempts to incriminate each other when Anne Newsome came to the door. "Inspector? Can I see you for a moment? Sergeant Bourke isn't in his office, and I've come up with something that might be important."

Carol surprised herself by regarding Anne's suppressed excitement with indulgent amusement. "Tell me about it."

"I've been checking through Bryce Darcy's things. He had a habit of writing telephone numbers, reminders, people's names, on the nearest piece of paper. So far most of them seem to have to do with work, or with the committees he was on. This morning, though, I found two things that were linked . . ."

Carol thought of herself as a young constable, and the dramatic pauses she had used before revealing a particularly startling item. She repressed a smile and made an encouraging sound. Passing her a booklet, Anne said, "You've probably seen this before. It was handed out on World AIDS Day to educate the public about the HIV virus and give people contact numbers. Bryce Darcy circled a number on the last page."

Carol turned to the back of the booklet where two pages contained a directory of information and support groups. The last item had a blue ink circle drawn firmly around it. The same blue pen had been used to doodle a series of interconnected boxes in the margin.

"What's a GAMMALINE?" asked Carol.

"It's a national information number for GAMMA, the Gay and Married Men's Association."

Carol put down the booklet. "I've never heard of them before. Have you?"

"Not until last year when one of my friends split up with his wife. He told me he'd had fleeting affairs with men for most of his married life and the only way he came to terms with being gay was through GAMMA."

Carol felt the ambivalence that always gripped her when someone mentioned another person's homosexuality. On one hand she felt a pulse of recognition — on the other the increasingly uncomfortable worry that she should say or do nothing to identify herself with that person. She said, "Are you telling me Bryce Darcy was bisexual?"

Anne leaned over the desk to give her a crumpled manila envelope. On the back two telephone numbers were written, along with the name *Steve*. "I found this envelope jammed in with other papers in his briefcase. I've been systematically checking out any telephone references and these are GAMMA numbers. The one in the AIDS booklet is an Australia-wide one where you get further information, but these two are specific to Sydney."

"They're private numbers?"

"Yes. I rang them both this morning, but only the one marked Steve answered. He didn't want to talk to me at first, but I've explained the situation in general terms, so he's willing to be interviewed."

"Did he speak to Bryce Darcy?"

"The system's set up to protect everyone's

privacy. First names only are used, so you can call and discuss everything quite freely with a man who's been through it too. Of course there's no guarantee anyone uses his real name and this guy Steve didn't remember a Bryce."

"I'd like to see him this morning. Is that possible?"

With a hint of complacent pleasure at her own efficiency, Anne said, "I've lined it up. He'll be in all morning and all I have to do is call and make a definite time."

* * * * *

Steve managed a medium-sized air freight company in Darlinghurst. In his late thirties, of average height and looks, he wore a mundane dark blue suit with white shirt and bland tie. He shook her hand, ushered her into his office, arranged for coffee — assuring her it was the genuine brew, not instant — and sat back to survey her with shrewd eyes.

"Do I pass muster?" asked Carol with a smile, thinking what an ordinary, pleasant man he looked. Then she was ashamed of herself. Why shouldn't he be ordinary and pleasant? After all, *she* didn't have *lesbian* printed across her forehead.

"You certainly do." He waited while a junior brought in two cups of coffee. "Now, Inspector, you wanted to ask me about someone named Bryce. I gather it's a murder investigation, and I've put two and two together and got Bryce Darcy. After all, it's

145

not a common name and his death's been in the news. It's the one where his sister was found with the body. Am I right?"

"Yes, but I'd appreciate it if you kept this confidential."

He grinned. "Confidentiality is one thing I can guarantee."

"You told Constable Newsome you didn't remember any man of that name calling recently."

"No, though he mightn't have used his real name. Many men don't. Also, Inspector, I've checked around other members of the GAMMA committee and no one recalls a Bryce."

She sipped her coffee, nodding her appreciation at its flavor. "You have a lot of calls, a lot of names, I suppose."

Steve smiled briefly. "More than you could imagine."

"How about a Harrison?"

He sat forward. "That strikes a definite bell. I spoke to a man calling himself Harrison several times."

"It's Bryce Darcy's middle name. Please tell me everything you can remember." When he hesitated, she said, "If Harrison *is* Bryce Darcy, then this aspect of his life is important because his involvement with your organization could put a whole new slant on our investigation. For example, the possibility now exists that he might have been killed by a male lover."

Steve still looked reluctant. "The things we discussed — he spoke openly, with complete frankness, never expecting them to be made public . . ."

"I'm sure," said Carol grimly, "that Bryce Darcy didn't expect to be murdered, either."

* * * * *

"When I phoned Wilma Darcy's sister I got the redoubtable Wilma herself," said Bourke, swerving into a gap in the stream of impatient traffic feeding onto the turgid Parramatta Road artery. "I regret to say she wasn't exactly gracious when I suggested we must see her again."

"Perhaps your charm is fading, Mark."

He grinned. "She's just too ultra-feminine for me, Carol. And now she's a widow, I'm wary of encouraging her."

Carol made a mocking rejoinder, but Bourke's words resonated in her. Wilma Darcy was the type of woman who would never be without a man. Her life's success was measured against the type and quality of the husband she snared and could display. Her self-esteem would be measured in other people's eyes, in society's appreciation of her achievements in attracting and keeping a suitable mate.

The black vinyl furniture in Darlene Fox's lounge room was still as stiffly uncomfortable, the copper ornaments retained their hectic shine. Wilma awaited their entry with a similar pale silence — but Carol sensed that something was different. It was as though Wilma had moved from the role of grieving wife to one of militancy. Her back was straight, her slight body tense, her triangular face set.

Without preamble, Wilma said, "I presume you're here because you've spoken to the counselor I saw the day Bryce died."

Carol had had a short phone conversation with the psychotherapist, who had confirmed the appointment and had made a few very general comments about the meeting. She could think of nothing he had said that would cause this beleaguered response. Hiding her surprise, she said, "Yes, I have spoken to him. Is there any comment you would care to make?"

"I thought they were like doctors — not allowed to discuss their patients' private affairs. Now that you're here, I realize I was wrong." Wilma's voice was suffused with bitterness.

Carol glanced at Bourke, who was maintaining a sympathetic expression. He sat down beside Wilma on the shiny blackness of the overstuffed couch. With a friendly smile, he said, "I know it's upsetting to have these private matters brought up, and normally we'd have no interest in what goes on between your counselor and yourself. But with your husband's murder, everything becomes important. In the long run, most of what we find out isn't relevant —"

"I can't see how my boys can have anything to do with it!"

Carol couldn't either, and she admired Bourke's response. "Perhaps we have the wrong slant on it . . ." His demeanor invited her to set him straight on the details.

Wilma, Carol was fascinated to see, looked embarrassed. "I suppose you'd think it rather premature, the boys being so young, but I was worried. Bryce wasn't a strong father, he didn't like disciplining them. He'd always indulge them, forgive them if they did something wrong. I'd read . . . well, if you have a dominant mother and a weak father . . ." She made a flustered gesture. "And it's when they're young the damage is done."

"That's true," said Bourke, nodding agreement.

"I needed professional advice. I'm like any mother, I just want Warren and Jonathan to have normal, happy lives. But with a father . . ."

As her voice trailed away, Carol gambled that she had grasped the situation correctly. She said, "Did Bryce actually tell you he had homosexual inclinations, or did you guess?"

Wilma's expression became pitiless. "He shouldn't have married me if he felt that way. He made a fool of both of us. When he told me, I felt physically sick. And the boys — if they find out — how can they live down the fact that their father wasn't . . . normal?"

Bourke's voice showed empathy. "And your fear is that there's a possibility they'll take after their father?"

Wilma glared at him resentfully. "Why are you bothering to ask me? You know what I discussed with the psychotherapist — the steps I could take to stop my children turning into queers."

* * * * *

Nora Darcy admitted Carol to her Hyde Park unit with a polite, tired smile. "Yesterday I was feeling rather stressed. I hope you'll forgive me if I was rude."

As Carol murmured an appropriate response she watched Nora Darcy closely. Wilma had said that her mother-in-law knew nothing about Bryce's homosexuality and had promised not to contact her.

149

Carol had little faith in Wilma's word, but Nora did seem reasonably relaxed and welcoming.

The Darcys' luxurious apartment was set high above the traffic noise, and afforded spectacular views of Sydney city and, in the distance, glimpses of the deep blue of the harbor. Toy cars and ant people hurried on their various ways, oblivious to those looking down from their angular glass balconies.

Hating to disturb Nora's peace, Carol made herself flatly state, "We have information that Bryce had homosexual relationships."

Nora's eyes widened at her words. "That's impossible. Worse — it's a disgusting suggestion."

Carol's voice was quiet, sure. "I'm afraid there's no doubt that your son approached GAMMA. The private details he gave during counseling sessions positively identified him."

"Identified him? Based on the word of a . . . *homosexual?*" said Nora.

Carol said nothing. Nora was restive, tugging at a drape, straightening a cushion. She turned back to Carol. "Does Keith have to know anything about this despicable allegation? He's been in Melbourne on business and is flying back this afternoon, so I presume he knows nothing about it as yet."

"I'm afraid your husband has to be told."

"But he'll be upset — revolted — that anyone could make such an accusation against Bryce." When Carol remained impervious to her plea, her attitude changed, her voice filled with outrage. "It's defamatory. I want the name of the man who made it."

To soothe her, Carol said sympathetically, "This must be upsetting for you —"

"Upsetting!" She glared at Carol. "Bryce is dead. He can't defend himself. Can you even begin to imagine what it feels like to have his name smeared with the suggestion he was homosexual?"

Carol's voice was compassionate. "You had no idea at all about this? Bryce never hinted, implied anything?"

With a motion of her hand Nora rejected Carol's words. "There was nothing to imply, because the whole thing's a lie, a fabrication," she said harshly. "Wilma mentioned she was seeing a counselor, but that isn't unusual. Many marriages have problems, and they can be ironed out." She stopped, tilted her head. "Has Eric Higgins got anything to do with this slander?" she demanded.

"No."

Nora's face was determined. "Bryce was happily married. He's got two little sons, and a loving wife. Does that sound like he's a deviate?"

Thinking of her own years as a member of the comfortable married majority, Carol said shortly, "He could have all those things, and still be gay."

Her comment stung. Nora's voice rose. "No! I would have known."

She persisted. "You never had any suspicion? The matter was never raised with you, even obliquely?"

"How many times do I have to say no?" asked Nora fiercely.

"If he didn't mention it to you, could he perhaps have confided in his father?"

Nora obviously found Carol's insistence galling. "I would have known if he'd said anything to Keith —

we have no secrets between us. And besides, if there was anything — and I'm telling you there couldn't be — Bryce would have come to me first."

Carol, hearing the tremor in these last words, spoke gently. "This is a recent thing. He's only been talking to members of GAMMA over the last month or so. The man who counseled him said Bryce had decided to tell you about it, but he was apprehensive about the reception he might have."

Nora's combativeness was exhausted. She sank down onto a floral couch, her shoulders slumped, her head down. "We brought Wilma and the boys down from the Mountains with us this morning. Have you asked her about it?"

"Yes."

"And surely she said it's nonsense, just as I have. And Carol, a wife should know."

Having spoken of this very point with Steve during their discussion that morning, Carol repeated his answer. "Not necessarily. Most wives of married men in this situation have no idea about the secret sexual life their husbands are leading. And of course there are some partners who prefer to pretend it doesn't exist, so they keep their suspicions to themselves."

Disgust twisted Nora's mouth. "But what about AIDS? Their wives would be at risk."

Before Carol could respond, a key turned noisily in the door and Keith Darcy strode into the room. In his gray striped suit he looked solid, prosperous, certain. He put down his bulging black briefcase and advanced to greet her. "Carol! I didn't expect to see you here. Have there been developments in the case? Do you have new information?"

Not wanting Nora to get in first, to sugar-coat the bitter pill so that the shock would be less, she said without ceremony, "We've evidence that a few weeks before his death Bryce contacted a gay support organization for married men who have homosexual inclinations."

She watched to see what effect her bald statement would have, wondering if he had already suspected his son's secret. Keith stared at her, incredulous, a flush rising under his already ruddy skin. "You're not trying to tell me Bryce was a queer?"

"I'm saying that he had several counseling sessions with GAMMA — the Gay and Married Men's Association."

Anger hardened his voice. "Bryce was as straight as the next man! He wasn't effeminate, a pansy!"

Nora rose, putting a restraining hand on his arm. He shook off the hand, advancing on Carol with hostility clear in the set of his heavy shoulders and his out-thrust chin. "This is obviously a slanderous attack by someone with an axe to grind. Where did you get the information? Did you check it out? Who told you?"

Without giving names, Carol briefly outlined Constable Newsome's discovery of the telephone numbers and her own subsequent questioning of the man Bryce had spoke to several times.

Keith Darcy responded with certainty. "It wasn't Bryce. It was someone using his name. Did this man actually say he was Bryce Darcy?"

"Only first names are used when contact is made. The man we believe was your son called himself Harrison."

He narrowed his eyes, brushed his mustache firmly with short strokes of his fingers. "Well, there you are, Carol. What more do you want? Obviously it wasn't my son."

Carol kept steady eye contact as she said, "Bryce's second name is Harrison. Also, there are just too many points of reference, too many details only your son would have known."

He shook his head slowly. "It's impossible." Taken by a sudden thought, he said, "There's something you haven't considered. Bryce must have been doing it for someone else, someone who wasn't game himself. My son was like that — he'd help people, even someone like that."

"If that is the case, can you suggest who this person might be?"

He shook his head fretfully. "How would I know? It's your job to find out. One thing you can bet — whoever it is won't come forward. You'll have to find him!"

CHAPTER ELEVEN

While Bourke set off to interview the psychotherapist Wilma Darcy had seen for advice on her children's sexuality, Carol visited Charlotte, who was still a patient at Naomi Reed's deluxe clinic.

Carol was glad to find Charlotte noticeably better. Her face had color, her eyes were clear and direct, and even her hair seemed to curl with greater vigor. Instead of the neutral colors of the last time, her clothes, casual slacks and matching top, were a bright tangerine.

We could be friends, thought Carol, pleased with

the uncomplicated warmth of Charlotte's greeting. Unwilling to raise a subject that might be upsetting, Carol chatted on inconsequential matters until Charlotte said, "Inspector, much though I would like it to be, I'm sure your visit isn't just a friendly one. Something's happened about Bryce."

Retreating into her official persona, Carol said, "Did you have any idea, any hint, that your brother might be gay?"

Charlotte didn't seem shocked by the question. She paused, then said, "I thought, sometimes . . . but no, Bryce never confided anything like that." She shook her head slightly, adding, "I did wonder, especially when we were younger. When he married Wilma I forgot about it."

Carol briefly explained about the contact he had made with GAMMA, then asked, "How would your family have reacted if your brother had come right out and said he believed he was gay?"

Charlotte smiled ruefully. "The conventional shock-horror, I suppose. My mother, in particular, abhors anything to do with homosexuality. My father, if the subject's ever come up, sees it as a sickness, with the person more to be pitied than condemned."

"He was very angry when I told him."

"Dad's what you'd call a man's man," Charlotte said with irony. "He'd think Bryce being gay was an unfortunate reflection on himself — that he'd failed as a father by not playing enough football with his son, or neglecting to take him shooting, or something masculine like that."

Curious, Carol said, "What do you think about it?"

Charlotte shrugged. "Me? I think it just happens — you're gay or not gay. I can't imagine anyone would deliberately *choose* to be, when you see what a hassle it is for most people." Her face grew serious. "Poor Bryce," she said softly.

"Looking back, he didn't have any special male friends? Anyone who might have had a close personal relationship with him?"

"How abstract you're being," said Charlotte with gentle mockery. "You mean, can I think of any gay relationships he might have had?"

Charlotte's humor faded as she considered the question. Her mouth tightened. "I can't believe what I'm thinking," she said. Carol remained silent, her eyes fixed on the other woman's face. Charlotte finally said, "Megan's father . . . he was one of my brother's closest friends."

"You're suggesting —"

Charlotte cut her off. "No. I'm almost sure there was no physical relationship between Bryce and Alex, but when I found I was pregnant, Bryce turned against Alex so strongly, he hated him so much. At the time I believed it was because I was his sister, and his best friend had got me into trouble . . . Now I wonder if Bryce was jealous, if he loved Alex, too."

Carol said, "I don't like asking you these questions," then wondered why she had said that. It was her job to probe, to dig, to relentlessly turn over every detail, every private fact that might have bearing on the crime she was investigating.

Charlotte seemed at ease. "Ask," she said. "If it helps find who killed Bryce, I don't mind what I have to answer."

157

Carol thought: She no longer thinks she's a suspect. Why is that?

Seeming to hear Carol's unspoken query, Charlotte added, "Of course, Inspector Ashton, I'm quite aware I must be somewhere near the top of your list of suspects, and when I saw you last I believed there was some possibility I might have attacked Bryce without knowing what I was doing. Now I don't believe that's true. I can visualize fragments of that dreadful afternoon — nothing that would help you, I'm afraid — but one thing I *do* remember clearly is coming into the workroom and finding Bryce already dead., I've gone over it again and again in my imagination and I'm sure he was killed before I got there."

Carol asked her to describe it frame by frame, as though watching a movie. Then took her through it again, asking her to experience each moment with all her senses. "For example, you may have heard something, or smelt something that you've forgotten . . ."

After twenty minutes Charlotte shook her head in frustration. "I'm sorry, it's all confused. I have an impression of raised voices, of an argument, then sudden silence, but I could be imagining it all."

"The voices? Both male? One a woman? Did you recognize your brother?"

Charlotte threw her hands up in frustration. "I can't be sure. When I try to recreate that afternoon, the colors and the sounds all melt into each other." She looked at Carol with candor. "You know I'd tell you if there was anything that would help."

Carol reminded herself that sincerity was the province of the effective liar, but this cautious

158

thought could not shake her belief that she was hearing the truth.

"If we can go back to when you were sixteen," she said more abruptly than she intended. "You were sent away when your family discovered you were pregnant."

Charlotte smiled wryly. "Yes, to stay with a rather remote cousin in England. All those years ago, it seemed a reasonable thing to do. Now — it strikes me as rather ridiculous. My father arranged everything, but Bryce, even though he was only seventeen or eighteen, was the prime mover. No one wanted the baby adopted out, so my mother spent most of my pregnancy with me, then brought Megan back to Australia with her, leaving me to follow some time later. She gave out the story that the baby belonged to close relatives living overseas who had been killed in an accident, and that Megan was going to be brought up as her own. I don't know how many people swallowed the story, but Megan certainly didn't know anything about it until she was quite old."

"She resented not being told the truth?"

"Very much." Charlotte's tone was regretful. "And quite unfairly she blames Bryce, though when it comes down to it, the decision was a family one. You mustn't think I was railroaded — I had a say, too, and went along with the idea."

"Megan's father — where is he?"

"After I was safely in England my father arranged with Alex's parents for him to leave the Blue Mountains. The arrangement was that my father would pay for Alex to finish his schooling in Melbourne and then, if he wished, go to university there. The one condition was that Alex would never try to communicate with me or with his daughter."

"Has he ever seen Megan?"

Pain shadowed Charlotte's face. "No. He drowned during a yacht race on Port Phillip Bay during his first year in Melbourne. He was only nineteen."

"You're sure of that?"

Charlotte smiled briefly at Carol's suspicion. "Alex's parents told me about his death and I believed them, but I'll give you the details if you want to check."

"Just routine."

"Funny," said Charlotte, "I knew you were going to say that."

* * * * *

As Carol was about to leave the air-conditioned cocoon of the clinic to face the blustery outside world, Naomi Reed came out of her office. "Inspector Ashton, if I might see you for a moment." Her clipped words carried effortlessly across the thickly carpeted hall.

She was attired almost exactly as before, her white medical coat cut in flattering lines, her gold jewelry expensively understated. Such constancy, Carol thought, had to be as deliberately created as the ambience of peaceful luxury that permeated the clinic itself.

It was apparent that Dr. Reed wanted to speak privately. She led Carol into her office, saying to her secretary, "Dawn, absolutely no interruptions, please. I'll be free in about twenty minutes."

Carol expected her to put the bulwark of her

desk between them, but Naomi Reed chose an adjacent peach-colored chair. "Inspector, I've been tossing up in my mind whether or not to contact you. I wasn't entirely frank before, I trust you'll understand why when I explain further."

Carol was both intrigued and puzzled. In their initial meeting Dr. Reed, as Charlotte Darcy's doctor, had been as forthcoming as could be expected under the circumstances.

Naomi Reed linked her fingers neatly, resting her hands on her lap. She looked perfectly in command of any eventuality, secure in her own quiet control. Regarding Carol with steady dark eyes, she said, "I would like your word, Inspector, that if what I'm about to tell you has no relevance to Bryce Darcy's murder, then it will go no further than this room."

"Of course."

"As I said, previously I wasn't entirely frank. Bryce certainly did come to me because he was worried about his sister, and I did give him the advice that I recounted to you. What I neglected to mention is that Bryce approached me as a patient himself."

Carol felt a sudden thrill of anticipation, as though something she would now hear would in some way realign the way she had been looking at the case. She waited silently.

"Bryce consulted me about six months before his death, and well before his concern about Charlotte's behavior. Perhaps you have an inkling of what I'm about to tell you, Inspector . . ."

"His homosexuality?"

Carol felt she'd passed some small test when Dr. Reed nodded acknowledgment. "Indeed. No doubt you

you found something in his papers — his family certainly didn't know. He said he'd been tormented — his word — for most of his adolescent and adult life by his physical attraction to other males. The Darcy family is basically patriarchal in structure, with Keith as the arbiter of family expectations of roles and acceptable behavior. As you must know, Keith also has a high public profile, not only as a successful businessman, but also because of the excellent work he has done with disadvantaged youth, particularly boys. In the early days Keith himself was personally involved in different youth programs, rather than just providing money and his name, as he does today. Keith made sure Bryce took part in various courses from his teens, taking him on two-week wilderness treks to build self-reliance and self-esteem with up to twenty or so boys who had come before the Children's Court for various offenses."

Carol said, "Is it important I know that Bryce was taken on these courses?"

"Yes, very. Bryce told me that during one of these treks he had his first homosexual experience with one of the other boys. Unfortunately Keith caught them in what could only be called a compromising position, and he beat Bryce severely. The other boy involved was ignored. Keith told Bryce that homosexuality was a weakness, and that he was sure Bryce had just been led astray, that he would grow out of it anyway — but he must realize that his mother would never forgive him if she knew."

Carol said, "Nora Darcy was very upset when I told her that Bryce had contacted GAMMA."

Dr. Reed gave a small, dry smile. "Nora is, if I

may say so as a private comment, a classic homophobe. She certainly had no idea that her own son might be suspect in that area. I'm sure Keith never told her, and Bryce repressed that part of his nature from that incident onward. After some years where he avoided emotional contact, except within the safety of his own family, he married and had children. But of course the mimicking of heterosexuality didn't make Bryce one. He remained homosexual, even though he had no physical relationship with another male."

Carol framed a question which she had asked herself many times. "Do you think homosexuality is innate?"

"I'm convinced that it is. To draw an analogy, homosexuality can be compared to left-handedness, or the ability to learn languages easily, or a talent for mathematics. It seems clear from historical records that quite independent of society's acceptance or persecution, at least ten percent of the population have always been homosexual. And it's as futile to try and change it as it is to alter any other innate quality."

Carol wanted to ask, Then why the hatred? Why the bashing? Why the rejection by society of part of its self? She said, "What had Bryce decided to do?"

"He came to me because he found the conflict between his true nature and the demands and standards of his family too much to endure. Add to that his distress because he loved his children and could see that he might be kept away from them. He thought his mother, in particular, would try to prevent his access to her grandchildren."

"But why?"

Dr. Reed smiled grimly. "He thought — and I agree with him — that his mother would believe he could corrupt his own children."

Carol was appalled at the inflexibility of such rejection. She had never met Bryce Darcy, but she felt close to him — as though his personality and the problems he had faced were those of a friend. She wondered if he had been unbearably unhappy in his last months of life. "Were you able to help him?" she asked, thinking how inadequate the question seemed. How did you help someone whose whole life might be destroyed because he chose to tell the truth about himself?

Dr. Reed said, "I treated him for depression and I referred him to GAMMA so he would be able to talk over his situation with men who understood it from their own experience."

"You mention his mother, Dr. Reed, and I can see her opinion was very important to him — but not his wife. Did you discuss how Wilma Darcy might react?"

With a dismissive gesture the doctor said, "His wife would want it hushed up, glossed over. Bryce thought Wilma would be angry and embarrassed, but then she would agree to a settlement and let her keep custody of the boys and maintain her lifestyle."

Carol smiled ironically at this summation of Wilma Darcy, but she felt there was more steel in Bryce's wife than Dr. Reed had allowed for.

Naomi Reed went on, "Bryce hoped his family would come to terms with the situation and wouldn't reject him completely. He was also relying on the fact that he had an integral role in Darcy Designs, quite apart from being an equal partner in the business along with his parents and sister."

Carol asked the question she had kept back at the beginning of their conversation. "Why have you decided to tell me this now?"

For the first time Naomi Reed showed some discomfiture. "With Bryce dead I persuaded myself it would only upset the family. But over the last few days I've thought about my last telephone conversation with him, and I believe I should have told you . . ."

Impatient at the pause, Carol snapped, "Told me *what?*"

"The week before he died Bryce called me. He said he believed he might be HIV positive. He asked me to arrange a blood test, but he died before it could be done."

Carol looked at her in astonishment. "You were there, with Bryce's body. There was blood, some of it on Charlotte Darcy. If there was any chance that Bryce was HIV positive, didn't it strike you as imperative that you warn everyone there?"

Naomi Reed looked away from her, and made no answer.

Carol added savagely, "It so happens that the post mortem showed he wasn't HIV positive — but you weren't to know that, were you, Dr. Reed?"

CHAPTER TWELVE

Mark Bourke's office desk was, as always, neat. Carol frowned at his in-tray, wondering how he managed to keep it under control when hers always bulged with material she kept promising herself to attack.

Bourke seemed uncharacteristically subdued. Carol said, "You okay?"

"I'm tired — had a very late night."

His tone invited comment, but Carol retreated. She needed to concentrate upon the case, to measure the scenario coalescing in her mind against the

evidence and the personalities. She said, "I want
Eric Higgins re-interviewed about the call he made
to the Darcys' apartment after finding Bryce's body.
I'm interested in who answered the phone, emotional
reactions to the news — every detail."

Bourke observed dryly, "Eric won't be at all
pleased to see me again." He yawned. "Anything
else?"

"Any progress on finding the psychiatrist Bryce
told Megan he was seeing that Monday?"

"Not a thing. I think, if he did see a specialist,
he used another name. I've tried Harrison and
combinations of family names, but came up with
nothing."

An idea occurred to Carol. She said, "Will you try
the gay support groups — ask for their hate-list of
medical practitioners who specialize in treating
homosexuality as a disease or personality disorder."

"All right, I'll get onto it. Meanwhile, here's Alex
Camody's death certificate and the coroner's report."
Bourke handed faxed documents to Carol. "Just as
Charlotte Darcy said, he died in Melbourne at
nineteen in a sailing accident."

"No chance it could be anything else?"

Bourke shook his head. "No, just a combination
of bad luck, poor judgment and a high sea."

Carol sat musing. At last she said, "I don't
understand why Bryce suddenly decided to leave a
collection of oil paintings to cousins he hardly knew.
I want someone to fly up to Brisbane and interview
the Darcy relatives there."

"Anne?"

Carol smiled. "Why not? She's bright enough to
ask the right questions." As she spoke, she realized

that the resentment she had felt towards Anne Newsome had dissolved, becoming irrelevant as her perspective had changed. She said, "Have you got anything on the valuations yet?"

Bourke was chagrined. "Carol, I'm sorry. I meant to ask Pat, but I didn't get around to it."

Carol knew her expression showed surprise. To neglect to follow through something like this was quite uncharacteristic of Bourke's usual painstaking approach. It suddenly occurred to her that his relationship with Pat might be rather more serious than she had thought. She said lightly, "Mark, you're not thinking of getting married, are you?"

Abashed, he ran his hand over his short hair. "It might be a possibility," he said.

Carol found herself at a loss. She said truthfully, "I don't know what to say."

He grinned. "Frankly, neither do I. It isn't anything I planned . . ."

Carol felt affection for him rise in her smile. "It is Pat, I trust?"

"Yes. But nothing's definite. It mightn't work out . . ."

Mark Bourke in love, she thought. The idea was so extraordinary, so warming, that she did something she had never done before. Leaning forward, she touched his hand. His fingers closed around hers.

She said, "Mark, I'm so pleased."

As they looked at each other awkwardly, Carol was aware that their relationship had undergone a subtle shift, and that some of the walls she had built she had allowed to be breached.

* * * * *

Carol spread the documents covering Bryce Darcy's murder across her desk. Finding the list of suspects, she scanned the names: Bryce's wife, Wilma; the Darcy family, Keith, Nora, Charlotte, Megan; Eric Higgins and Janice Russo.

She began to doodle a series of elaborate arrows as she considered each person.

Wilma Darcy: Poor girl made good, using marriage to give her the prestige and money she so ardently desired. What would she be willing to do to preserve the life she had achieved? Would Wilma consider honorable widowhood preferable to being the discarded wife of a homosexual? She had the opportunity, as her appointment with the counselor concluded at one o'clock — she knew her husband would be at his sister's place — and she possessed the requisite steel in her character.

Keith Darcy: Patriarch of the family, driving force behind Darcy Designs and widely known for his involvement in youth work. He had been deeply grieved at Bryce's death, and in any case, why would he kill the son who was clearly so important to the company's marketing strategies? His wife said she had found him resting in their city apartment when she returned from shopping in the early afternoon . . . but of course that created an alibi for her, too. What if one were covering for the other?

Nora Darcy: Dr. Reed had called her a classic homophobe — had she known about her son's homosexuality earlier? If so, was such knowledge enough to drive her to destroy him? Certainly there was a formidable, unbending side of her personality that was usually hidden.

Charlotte Darcy: She had the opportunity, the

weapon was hers, the location her studio, her brother's blood was on her clothes. But she had been drugged to the point of psychosis — a perfect person to set up as guilty of an unpremeditated killing because she was unable to defend herself from the accusation.

Megan Darcy: Resentful and difficult, she blamed Bryce for the confusion of her early life, but surely that was not enough motive to attack him with a hammer. Add the fact that her presence at tutorials and lectures the afternoon her uncle died gave her a reasonable alibi, and she had to be relegated to the bottom of the list of suspects.

Eric Higgins: A businessman with a string of failures — and Charlotte Darcy was his meal ticket. He was not popular with his wife's family — both Nora and Megan were keen to blame him for Bryce's death. He was certainly guilty of drugging his wife, with no thought to the misery and fear she would experience. And he had sound motives for removing his brother-in-law, including the fact that Bryce was threatening to cut off the money and that he also knew about Janice Russo — a lever that might be used to break up a financially fruitful marriage.

Janice Russo: More an accessory than a major player? But why give her a subsidiary role? She seemed quite capable of ruthless action. She could be the driving force that propelled Eric into action, or perhaps she had taken the initiative herself. And her motive? Love? Sex? Power over a weak man? All three?

Carol glanced over the names again, then turned to a tentative timetable of Bryce Darcy's movements on the day he died. He had left Katoomba at approximately nine o'clock in the morning, taking at least an hour and a half to reach Sydney. Presuming his appointment with the unknown psychiatrist was in the city, this had to be scheduled somewhere between ten-thirty and eleven-thirty to give him time to consult with the doctor and then drive to his sister's place, arriving at one o'clock.

He was murdered between two and three, probably at approximately two-thirty, so there was at last an hour before he died.

Eric Higgins claimed to have returned home at about three-thirty to find his wife sitting by her brother's body. He called his in-laws' city apartment, then the emergency services, the call being logged at three-fifty. The first police on the scene arrived at four o'clock. Keith and Nora Darcy, accompanied by Dr. Naomi Reed, appeared at six, shortly after Mark Bourke and Anne Newsome had arrived on the scene.

Carol scribbled a note to herself: *Dr. Reed — whose idea was it to bring her?*

Bourke put his head through the doorway. "You were right about contacting gay support organizations — we've got the psychiatrist Bryce saw on Monday morning. A Dr. Roderick Chernside. He was second on the gay avoid-at-any-cost list and specializes in aversion therapy."

Carol was impelled to her feet by the exhilaration of the breakthrough. "You sure the patient was Bryce Darcy?"

"Absolutely. He used the name Bryce Graham, but the description, details of life — everything fits. And Carol, a fascinating thing . . . a woman made the appointment for him."

* * * * *

As Carol was briefing Anne Newsome for her trip to Brisbane, Bourke burst into the room. "Sorry to interrupt, but you're just not going to believe what I've got on those paintings Bryce Darcy left to his Uncle Walter's family."

"I think I can guess," said Carol. "I imagine the paintings are very valuable. Yes?"

He nodded. "Right on, Carol. They're early Australian impressionist — one's even an Arthur Streeton — and on the open market they should be worth the best part of a million dollars, maybe more."

Carol smiled. "And you're wondering why Bryce Darcy should leave such valuable paintings to relatives he hardly knows . . ."

"I sure am."

"I think," said Carol, "it's a question of guilt."

He shook his head. "Some guilt."

"Mark, you'll probably need a court order, but I want access to financial and legal records of Darcy Designs going back to before Walter Darcy died."

"No doubt, Carol, you want all this immediately, plus an expert opinion on the books, so you'd better tell me exactly what we're looking for."

"A dark family secret," said Carol flippantly. Then, more seriously, "And one that led to murder."

* * * * *

Dr. Naomi Reed's phone call was brisk and to the point. Carol had asked her to advise when Charlotte Darcy was leaving the clinic.

Understandably, Charlotte did not intend to return to her home with Eric Higgins, so her parents had arranged to pick her up early the next day to take her back with them to Katoomba.

Carol said, "In confidence, Dr. Reed, I'd like your opinion on certain forms of psychiatric treatment."

As she spoke she was wryly aware that she had the advantage. Naomi Reed would cooperate with any request because Carol knew about her failure to advise that Bryce Darcy's blood might be infected with the HIV virus.

She asked her questions, then said, "Dr. Reed, one more thing . . . who asked you to attend the murder scene and assess Charlotte's state of mind?"

She smiled grimly at Naomi Reed's answer but none of her satisfaction was reflected in her voice as she thanked the doctor for her assistance.

CHAPTER THIRTEEN

"Anne did a good job in Brisbane," said Bourke as he accelerated past a lumbering truck.

Carol felt as pleased as Bourke sounded. "Yes, she did. She's got a lot of promise and you've been right to extend her."

He smiled at the acknowledgment, but didn't make the jocular remark she expected. He said, "Carol, correct me if I'm wrong, but you seem . . . happier." He frowned. "I'm not putting this very well, but what I mean is I don't come in to work every morning expecting to find you've resigned."

"Yes, I feel better about things, Mark — but I'm not sure why."

"It's obvious to me you've just experienced an early mid-life crisis." He grinned. "A *very* early one, of course."

Carol thought, What's it in me that's changed? Is it that I've begun to realize that letting go doesn't mean the center of my world will give way? She looked at Bourke's blunt profile. Conscious of her gaze he flicked her a glance and quirked the corner of his mouth. She said, "Mark, would you and Pat be free for a barbecue next weekend? I haven't mentioned it to Sybil, but if she's available . . ."

That wasn't so hard, she thought, pleased by the alacrity with which he accepted the invitation.

As they grew closer to Katoomba her thoughts became focused on the case. She rehearsed with Bourke the strategies they would use, both conscious that the evidence they currently had was not conclusive.

Bourke, always cautious, said, "You know the legal details and the financial analysis of Darcy Designs is just a preliminary report . . ."

"It'll be enough," she said flatly, realizing that she felt the implacability of an avenger. This is for you, Bryce, she said silently to a man she had never met.

When they drew up in front of the Darcy mansion, Bourke gave a low whistle as he appraised the gray walls and incongruous glass outcrops of the building squatting in its huge landscaped gardens. His derision echoed Carol's own first impressions: "This may be Keith Darcy's masterpiece, but it convinces me he should stick to the business side of things."

Splintered glass colors scintillated as Megan Darcy opened the front door. She was her usual taciturn self, leading them with the minimum of grace through to the back of the house. Half of the large room was a conservatory, the glass letting in the slanting rays of the setting sun to light in brilliance ferns, palms and a range of orchids. The rest of the room was furnished with casually arranged matching sofas, lounges and chairs covered in a startling black and white irregular pattern. There were several black marble coffee tables, each bearing a brightly flowering plant in a black ceramic pot.

Carol, acknowledging recognition from the occupants of the room, quickly checked who was there. Megan, dressed carelessly in an ancient dark red sweater and faded jeans, stood smoking silently, in impatient endurance.

Keith Darcy seemed to seethe with suppressed emotion. His short graying hair sprang from his scalp with energy, his mustache bristled militantly, his color was high, his eyes glittered. Even the tailored excellence of his country-gentleman clothes seemed somehow awry. He moved jerkily towards Bourke and Carol, shook hands briefly, then, after a few staccato remarks, returned to sit by Nora's side.

Nora Darcy looked wary, but, Carol thought, somehow prepared. Wearing orange and brown culottes of some heavy material that had a surface sheen, she sat upright, feet together, hands clasped on her knees.

In contrast, Wilma Darcy in widow-black, her moist lips red with heavily applied lipstick, her fingers bearing a selection of rings, reclined with negligent ease, one arm along the back of the sofa, the angle of her head indicating a weary resignation.

Carol said, "Is Charlotte joining us?"

Megan responded as though eager to leave, stubbing out her half-smoked cigarette as she said rapidly, "She's upstairs, resting. I'll get her."

In the silence that followed, Carol heard Nora take a deep breath. Then she said, "Inspector, you've told us this is about Bryce. Does that mean you know what happened?"

Keith stroked his mustache furiously, then dropped his hand. "You're not going to arrest Charlotte, are you? I can't believe you'd let us bring her home, just to take her away again."

Carol kept her tone formal. "Important evidence has come to light in the last day or so. For example, we now believe we have a clear picture of Bryce's last hours."

As Carol was speaking, Charlotte, with Megan at her side, entered the room. Her eyes met Carol's and she smiled faintly. She was composed, the pallor of her face accentuated by the pearl gray sweater she wore.

His daughter's arrival galvanized Keith. He strode to her side, taking her arm protectively as he turned to Carol. He said harshly, "You've arrested Eric for trying to poison Charlotte, but you didn't charge him

177

with Bryce's murder. I want to know why he's off the hook. A man like that — he'd be capable of anything."

His accusing words hung in the air.

Carol looked at Bourke, who said, "On the day he died Bryce left Katoomba at nine o'clock and drove to Sydney to keep an appointment in the city at eleven with a psychiatrist, Dr. Roderick Chernside. He had never seen the doctor before and hadn't made the appointment himself. If fact, the receptionist believed that the woman making the arrangements was the secretary of someone called Bryce Graham."

Nora interrupted. "Bryce would have seen Naomi if he'd needed advice. Why would he go to this Dr. Chernside?"

Bourke had his answer ready. "Because this particular psychiatrist specializes in aversion therapy, where the patient endures some unpleasant punishment, such as an electric shock, in order to cure him or her of an obsession."

"I don't understand," said Wilma petulantly, sitting up straight on her sofa.

Carol raised her eyebrows. "I find that surprising, since you almost certainly made the appointment for your husband."

Wilma's expression was studied boredom. Shrugging elaborately, she turned her head away from any further involvement.

Carol glanced at Bourke, who moved to the center of the room as he said, "Bryce was persuaded to go to Dr. Chernside to discuss treatment for his homosexuality." Ignoring Nora's protesting exclamation he continued, "This particular psychiatrist belongs to a shrinking minority in the medical fraternity who believe that homosexuality is a personality disorder and that the patient's behavior can be modified by punishment."

Charlotte said, "That's barbaric!"

Bourke nodded agreement. "It seems that was your brother's view too. He made it clear that he completely rejected the doctor's analysis of homosexuality and that he had no intention of submitting to any type of aversion therapy. He then left the psychiatrist's office to drive to Charlotte's house in Baulkham Hills. It's likely that as soon as he arrived he either made or received a telephone call, during which he said that he wouldn't be going ahead with any treatment designed to 'cure' his homosexuality."

Nora was on her feet. "Don't keep saying that!" she exclaimed, her voice shrill. "Bryce wasn't homosexual, and nothing you can say will persuade me he was."

Keith, his heavy head down, hadn't moved, but he said indistinctly, "Nora, please . . ."

Charlotte moved to go to her mother, but Megan was quicker, taking her grandmother's arm and helping her back to her seat.

Carol waited, thinking how apprehension and stress could be used to erode the staunchest resolve. She took up the narrative. "Finding his sister confused and incoherent, Bryce stayed, probably expecting her husband would soon be home. During the next hour his murderer arrived to find him alone in Charlotte's studio. There was an argument and then, when his back was turned, Bryce was struck with a hammer snatched up from the workbench." She paused, her glance flickering over each person before she added quietly, "It only took two blows to kill him."

Nora's voice had a hysterical edge. "It was Eric Higgins. No one in the family — it couldn't be!"

Carol continued confidently, "We know that Charlotte's husband had given her a considerable dose of amphetamines that morning in her breakfast orange juice. At the time of the murder she was therefore suffering the symptoms of amphetamine intoxication, although she does have some valuable snatches of memory." A pause to let them absorb the idea that Charlotte might have remembered something vital, then Carol said, "Shortly after Bryce was killed, she entered the studio and found his body. She was still there when Eric Higgins returned home."

"So who murdered Uncle Bryce?" demanded Megan, brittle with tension. She drew hard on her cigarette, blowing out the smoke in a defiant stream. "We all know you think it's one of us, or you wouldn't be here."

Carol made a slight gesture to Bourke, who said conversationally, "One of the motives for Bryce's murder goes back many years to the time when his uncle, Walter Darcy, died. Walter's widow, Edna, was persuaded to sign over all her rights in the company. In return her brother-in-law guaranteed an allowance for life and funds to bring up her three young children. There was a proviso — she was to move north to Brisbane and cut any close ties with the family in Katoomba."

Keith lifted his head to eye Bourke coldly. "Is that why you've been bothering my accountants? I would have told you anything you needed to know." Narrowing his eyes, he said, "And there's nothing wrong with the agreement, if that's what you're trying to imply. Edna isn't a bright woman and she wasn't interested in the business. Add to that the fact that she came from Brisbane originally, and it's obvious she did what she wanted to do."

His attention switched to Carol as she said, "The solicitor who drew up the documents has a clear memory of the transfer, partly because he thought it an unusual agreement. He remembers that your sister-in-law hesitated when given the final papers to sign, and you said to her, 'It was Walter's idea that you do this, Edna, not mine.' "

Chin thrust forward, elbows locked, ready to heave himself out of the softness of the couch's cushions, Keith said, "You're trying to make something out of nothing. Walter and I agreed that if anything happened to one of us, the other would look after his brother's family." He glared at Carol. "And that's what I did. Edna and her children have never wanted for anything."

"So, in essence, your brother's family has been totally dependent upon your generosity and if you were to decide to terminate the annual grant then they would have nothing?"

Keith waved his hand as if to swat an insect. "These are mere details. The point is that I did what Walter asked me to do — I looked after his wife and children."

Bourke interposed, "Obviously your son Bryce also felt some responsibility for his aunt and cousins. In fact, he took a quick trip to Brisbane in June to see them."

"But my brother hardly knew them," said Charlotte, frowning. "I can only remember us meeting a few times when we were children, and Bryce hasn't mentioned them for years."

"Perhaps you're not aware that in his will your brother left them a collection of paintings."

An irritated exclamation from Wilma captured everyone's attention. "Just what is the point of all this, Inspector? Bryce had some paintings in storage. I don't think they were even insured. What does it matter what he did with them?"

"Some are rather valuable," said Bourke.

Nora, shaking off her husband's restraining hand, demanded, "How valuable?"

"Preliminary valuation puts them at the best part of a million dollars."

Carol was amused to see Wilma Darcy stiffen with surprise. Nora's reaction, however, was anger. A flush staining her pale cheeks, she exclaimed, "Not the Arthur Streeton? He couldn't have included that — it wasn't his to give!"

Carol said, "I understand that particular painting was legally deeded to your son on his twenty-first birthday."

Almost querulous, Nora said, "But only on the understanding Bryce keep it in the immediate family. He was to pass it on to his children, not to give it away."

Megan moved impatiently, the dancing patterns of smoke from her cigarette catching the last sunlight through the conservatory glass. "Look, where's this leading to? So Uncle Bryce sees his long lost relatives and decides to remember them in his will. So what?"

Bourke spread his hands. "His sudden interest in relatives he had only seen infrequently coincided with consultations he had with Darcy Designs' accountants and legal advisors. Why would that be?"

Charlotte spoke slowly, reluctantly. "It seems to me that Bryce thought Aunt Edna had been given a bad deal, so he was trying to make it up to her." She looked to her father. "Did you know about this? Why didn't Bryce say anything to me?"

Carol moved to stand directly in front of Nora where she sat rigidly beside her husband. "The good name of the Darcy family means a great deal to you, doesn't it?"

Nora stared up at her blankly. "Of course."

"And if Bryce made this public — the suggestion that your husband swindled your sister-in-law — there would be gossip, a scandal . . ."

"It isn't true!"

"And how could you be sure he wouldn't eventually believe he had to do something more immediate to right the wrong he thought had been done?"

Nora looked away, repeating almost listlessly, "It isn't true."

Keenly aware that the tension in the room was intensifying, Carol spoke slowly, distinctly. "You knew your son was gay, Nora."

Nora shook her head in denial, her face blotched redness against the orange and brown of her clothing.

Carol let the moment resonate, then said with firm emphasis on each word. "You knew Bryce was a homosexual."

Tears began to spill down Nora's trembling

cheeks. Charlotte, in protest, said to Carol, "Must you?"

Keith, putting his arm around his weeping wife's shoulders, demanded, "Why are you doing this? You know she can't cope."

Inexorable, Carol said to Nora, "Why was it *you*, not your husband, who made the call to Naomi Reed after Eric Higgins rang to say Bryce was dead? You were waiting to hear, weren't you? You already knew that Charlotte would be blamed."

Nora looked appalled. "No, that's not why . . . Keith was too upset —"

Carol interrupted, "So you were quite prepared for what you would see when you arrived at Charlotte's studio with your husband and Naomi Reed. In fact you were so calm that you assisted Sergeant Bourke when Keith came close to collapse after seeing your son's dead body."

Nora lifted her hand in entreaty. "How can you say that . . ."

Carol, intending there be no time for deliberation, said rapidly, "Charlotte was at risk, wasn't she? You knew she'd be accused of her brother's murder, so you brought in Dr. Reed to get her safely away to a clinic. With Charlotte out of circulation, you did your best to turn the blame onto Eric Higgins. And in case that didn't work, you made a private approach to me to have any possible charge against Charlotte reduced to manslaughter."

"Why would my mother kill Bryce?" cried Charlotte.

Concentrated on Nora, Carol said, "Wilma confided in you why she was seeing a counselor."

Nora moved her hands aimlessly. "Wilma? I never

184

spoke to Wilma. Keith told me they had a little trouble, nothing serious."

Looking down at the ravaged face of Bryce's mother, Carol knew the outcome depended upon how she wielded the power contained in her next questions. She said conversationally, "Nora, what do you think about homosexuality?"

"It's disgusting. It's unthinkable."

"And if your son had been homosexual . . . would he have deserved to die?"

Nora threw her head back, staring wordlessly at her. Carol could feel the air singing with tension and knew this was the point where she won — or lost.

Keith heaved himself out of the soft cushions, electric with rage. "How dare you do this!"

Carol didn't flinch, although his physical presence swelled with barely checked violence. She said, "We have strong evidence of both motive and opportunity."

He made a chopping motion with his hand. "It was all under control — now you do this. I can't allow it to continue."

Carol thought: He's so proud of his authority, his supremacy over people and events. She said, "I'm afraid it's nothing to do with you. Your wife is responsible —"

"No. I will not allow you to accuse her of Bryce's death. She had nothing to do with it."

"Dad?" Charlotte breathed into the silent room.

Carol repeated, "We have strong evidence."

Keith burned with furious contempt. "Evidence? You don't understand. Bryce wanted to destroy everything — his mother's happiness, his marriage,

185

even me, his father." His voice swelled with denunciation. "He refused to see the twisted sickness in him that had to be got rid of, one way or the other. He ignored his responsibilities to me and to his own family."

"Oh, Jesus," said Megan.

All Carol's certainties had gathered into this moment in the slowly darkening room. She glanced at Bourke, who moved unobtrusively to the periphery of the group. Then she said quietly, soothingly, "Tell me."

Keith's bearing was imperious, his voice authoritative. "Action had to be taken. Wilma came to me, as the head of the family, and told me Bryce had confessed that he had homosexual urges. She agreed with me that everything had to be kept quiet, for the boys' sake, if for no other reason." His lips thinned in anger as he shook his head. "In some way she must have failed him as a wife, otherwise why would he go out seeking this depravity?"

Wilma snapped, "You made him queer, not me!"

Ignoring the comment, he said to Carol firmly, "It was clear I had to do something about the situation."

Nora was watching her husband as though mesmerized. "Keith?" she said.

He seemed not to hear, speaking to Carol as if she were the only other person present. "You'd understand how relieved I was when Bryce agreed to see Dr. Chernside. I knew that treatment for his sickness would mean there was a good chance he would be cured and lead a normal life."

Charlotte touched his arm. "Dad, it's not a disease."

Charlotte touched his arm. "Dad, it's not a disease."

Carol thought: He isn't trying to persuade me he's right — he's telling me he is.

His expression severe, unforgiving, Keith continued, "But then Bryce called me from Charlotte's place and told me he rejected any therapy. I wanted to see him face to face, but he wouldn't leave his sister. I told him to wait there and I'd join him."

"And you found Bryce alone in the studio?"

Keith looked austere, autocratic. "I said to him, 'You're my son. Why are you doing this to me?' I explained that his mother would start drinking again, his children would suffer, everything I'd built for the family would be destroyed. Bryce didn't listen to me. He said his life was a lie, he wanted to set things right."

He waited but when she was silent he demanded, "Carol, you can see it was impossible, can't you? Not only did Bryce want to force me to accept his deviant behavior, he wanted me to give back a share of the company to Edna and her children because he thought I'd cheated them." He shook his head. "He refused to understand that what I'd done was simply good business practice."

Carol said softly, "But what made you kill him?"

A burning anger suffused his voice. "Understand this — I was willing to give him one last chance to change. Do you think I wanted him to die? I told him he was my son and I loved him. But it was obvious he wanted to taunt me, hurt me. He shouted at me, 'Would you love me, Dad, if I had AIDS?'"

Keith let his breath out in a long sigh, clasping his hands as if in prayer. "I knew then that I was looking at a stranger. It wasn't my son . . . it wasn't Bryce. And when he turned away, dismissing me, saying he was going to have a blood test for the virus, I picked up the hammer and I hit him. He fell and I hit him again. I had to. He wasn't my son anymore."

Carol gazed at him, her face expressionless. This was the patriarch who had judged his son and then executed him — yet had been so affected by what he had done that he'd been unable to answer the telephone when he knew what message was coming. This was the man who had demanded to view Bryce's body, only to collapse when he saw it. And now, here he stood, the pitilessly avenging father, godlike in his armored certitude.

Nora, her face slack, said hoarsely, "You killed our son?"

He seemed coldly incredulous at his wife's question. "He didn't deserve to live. In your heart you know that."

There was a frozen moment when, it seemed to Carol, time stretched to encompass the enormity of the realization that those in the room shared.

Then, shattering against Keith's calm invincibility, a wail broke from Nora, rising, trembling in the echoing silence: "My *son!*"

CHAPTER FOURTEEN

The midday sun warmed Carol's shoulders as she stood in her sheltered garden gazing meditatively at the fire blazing in the pit of the sandstone barbecue. Her eyes on the dancing orange-red flames from the eucalyptus wood, she went over each step of the scene that she had so carefully orchestrated to reveal Keith Darcy's guilt.

But she knew he didn't consider himself guilty. To him the death of his son was an execution, a just retribution for degenerate evil.

She felt again the full force of Keith Darcy's

unyielding hatred. It could have been me, she thought. I could have been the focus for that irrational, murderous hostility because of what I am.

For a moment a gray depression filled her. Bryce had hidden the reality of his nature, as she had. And when he had tried to proclaim his true self, he had been killed for it.

A sudden movement caught her attention. A little honey-eater, full of eager life, his scarlet breast brilliant in the sunlight, his beating wings blurring, hovered over a winter-flowering bush. With a flash of insight she realized there was a balance — for every person like Keith or Nora there was the loving warmth of an Aunt Sarah or the friendship of a Mark Bourke. And within the poisoned atmosphere of the Darcy family — both Megan and Charlotte.

Rising in her came a determination, a strength long denied. Soon I'll be willing to test the world, she thought. And if I find it wanting, I'll try to change it.

Her meditation was broken by Sybil, who had joined her in contemplation of the barbecue fire. Carol said, "Do you think it needs more wood?"

"Not unless you want to present Mark and Pat with a burnt offering."

Carol glanced at her watch. "They're late. Perhaps they're not coming."

Sybil put an arm around her waist and squeezed her. "I love you when you're anxious — maybe because it hardly ever shows."

Car doors slammed in the street level above them. "They're here," said Sybil. She sighed at Carol's tight expression. "Carol, don't try and control everything. Just relax and you'll have a good time."

She smiled mischievously. "Just the other night you had some practice at that, remember?"

"Oh, God," said Carol, laughing as she turned to go up to meet Mark Bourke and Pat, "not surrender *again?*"

Visit

Bella Books

at

BellaBooks.com

or call our toll-free number

1-800-729-4992